Simply Twisted

The Tenth Anniversary Edition

A collection of short stories, general
musings, poetry, and other
randomness...

by

Damien Smethurst

Cover photo printed with the permission of Valentin Padurean

Table of Contents

Introduction

Ten years ago I got it into my head that it would be really cool if I published a book. In my twisted mind it gave me a perfect chance to make every female member of my family cry on Christmas Day, without getting into trouble for it. This, I think, deep down, is how guys always think when nobody is paying attention to them. But that could just be me...

Anyway, that was then, and this is now, and those of you that got the original book are probably wondering, quite fairly to be honest, why you should get this one as well. What is it about this, the Tenth Anniversary Edition, that sets it apart from the original Simply Twisted book?

Well, there are a few things...

Firstly, I've actually made an effort to edit the stories this time, instead of just doing the cut and paste of first drafts of stories that I did originally. This means that a lot of the stupid mistakes in the first book have been excised and disposed of appropriately, although I doubt I got all of them so don't panic if you're the kind of person that enjoys seeing where someone messed up in their book.

Secondly, there are a bunch of stories and poems in this book that didn't make it the first time round, mostly because I hadn't written them at that time. There are also some notes at the back of the book explaining roughly what might have been going through my mind at the point of writing everything that's in this book. Except this introduction, as the only thing going through my mind right now is a vague hope that I'm getting close to the end of the page and can stop with this...

Anyway, for those that haven't been here before, you might want to know what this is all about...

It's simple enough really. Ever since I was a kid I've been fascinated with words and their relationship with one another, and sometimes, often when I least expect it, those words seem to become fascinated with me and use my brain and fingers to escape out into the world, hopefully to a place where they can be enjoyed by as many people as possible.

So I took some of my short stories, ramblings, and poetry, and put them all in a book for everyone to read.

Will you find classic literature between these pages?

Not really, no. But hopefully there will be something in here that everyone, regardless of what style or genre they generally like, can get a kick out of.

So sit back, grab your drink of choice, and relax. We're going to go on a little journey together. It's an odd journey, but not dangerous at least, and I look forwards to seeing you all out there on the other side.

Sunday Afternoon Drive

It started off as nothing more than a leisurely Sunday afternoon drive. My friend and I were bored, had nothing else to do, looked out of the window at a beautiful day, and decided to just jump in the car and see where we ended up.

So we drove, and we drove, and then we drove some more. We were having such a fun time, just laughing and joking, not paying much attention to what was going on around us, and the next thing we actually noticed was that we'd somehow managed to traverse half of Europe and were in Prague.

I have no idea how we got there, and my friend couldn't understand either. Neither of us had any recollection of doing any of the things you'd really need to do in order to drive across Europe, such as re-fuelling the car, getting on either a boat or going through the channel tunnel, or anything else. We couldn't even remember taking any toilet breaks.

A quick inspection of our wallets also showed what we both suspected, which is that we hadn't spent any money anywhere. This didn't make sense. We had a quick discussion and decided that the way forwards was to park the car up, book into a hotel somewhere, then go and get drunk while we tried to work out what had happened.

So we did just that.

The only place we could find to stay was a hostel, and all they had vacant were two beds in a four-bed room, with the other two beds in the room being already taken. We had no idea who our roommates were, but that wasn't a priority. Getting beer was the priority.

So we went out, as guys who are confused are liable to do. And before long we were pretty drunk. We weren't steaming drunk, or at least I wasn't, but we'd certainly knocked back quite a few beers between us. I noticed my friend was wobbling a fair bit though and decided that getting back to the room was now the main mission in hand.

We made light work of the trip back to the hostel, mainly because the bar we were in was next door. Finding our room was also quite easy, as we asked at reception and someone was kind enough to guide us all the way, and that's when we met our roommates for the night.

And very attractive roommates they were too. We were sharing with two young girls from Germany who had decided to travel around Europe in their holidays, who by some quirk of fate ended up sharing a room in Prague with two drunken guys from England who had decided to go for a Sunday afternoon drive.

The conversation was brief, mainly due to how drunk my friend and I were, and before long everyone had said good night and crawled into their respective beds to go to sleep. And sleep didn't take long to arrive.

It only seemed like a few moments later when I was awoken by a piercing scream. I looked towards the sound of the noise and noticed my friend standing over one of the German girls. I really have no idea how he could have become so confused, as he was generally quite bright and she was a very attractive young lady, but he appeared to have mistaken her for a urinal and was relieving himself all over her.

I shouted at him to try and get him to stop, and as he turned around to see where the shouting was coming from he managed to fill the poor girls shoes as well. I jumped out of my bed and forced him out of the door, then spent the next half an hour apologising many times and profusely to the two young ladies before going back out to try and find my errant friend.

And find him I did. Three floors up from the one we were staying on and curled up outside somebody's bedroom door, wearing nothing but his rather damp underpants and fast asleep. I carried him back to our room, which the two German girls had for some reason decided to vacate, and put him back into bed.

The next morning he had no recollection of the urinating incident, but he could recall walking around knocking on doors at random and asking the people behind them whether he lived there or not. For some reason, when we came to check out that afternoon we were informed in no uncertain terms that we were not welcome at that hostel ever again.

And to think, it all started off as nothing more than a leisurely Sunday afternoon drive.

Taken

How come they don't realise?

I've been watching the two of them for several days now. Everywhere they've been I've been right behind them, following them around. I suppose the textbook definition of what I've been doing would be stalking them.

Every place they go, I'm there as well, twenty four hours a day, making notes of every move that they make. I'm there in the shadows, always following closely behind them, just waiting for the right moment to arrive, as I know it surely must. It isn't the right time yet, but I sense that my chance is drawing close.

I'm sure now that at some point in the next couple of days my opportunity will present itself. It always does. I just have to be patient and wait for the right set of circumstances, and when the chance finally comes there is only ever one outcome.

Taken.

I've followed them into a nightclub now and can see them, just standing there, neither of them with a care in the world. They still have no idea that I'm watching them, hunting them down. I reach behind me for my drink, and when I turn back around I can see the two of them dancing. One of them is very good, and seems to know all the right moves. It's the blonde one, of course; blondes always seem to know how to dance.

But one thing the blonde doesn't know about is me. I'm there, behind them both always. I'm kind of surprised that they haven't noticed anything by now though as I've been tailing them for nearly 5 days. Maybe it's the alcohol, dulling their senses and making them feel invincible. Soon, though, they'll find out that there's no such thing as invincible.

They're both dancing together now, the blonde and the red-head, and I can see them grinding their bodies against one another, fondling each other. Obviously they mean it as a turn on, with both of them vying for attention from the men in the club. And it's working. Every guy in the place is looking at them getting down and dirty together on the dance-floor. One guy approaches the red-head and asks for a dance, but he walks away a few seconds later, clearly dejected.

One thing that I've noticed in the time that I've been following them is that they like to flirt with the guys, and sometimes even go as far as kissing some of them. The pair of them clearly see nothing wrong in accepting drinks off the guys whenever offered either. Always though, every time, they end up back together, holding each other and kissing. These two are a couple for sure.

Or is it just a tease, designed to turn the guys on? I'm not convinced either way.

It's a couple of hours later, and I can still see them. They're in a taxi now, heading for home, and I notice that they're no longer kissing and cuddling now there are no guys around to watch them. It's one of the things that makes me doubt they're really a couple.

The next night I trail them to a different club, but apart from that it's the usual routine for them, at first anyway. They head straight out onto the dance floor and start strutting away as though they own the place. Once again, they quickly have the attention of every guy in the place. And just like most nights, they quickly pair off with guys, starting the heavy flirting and dancing that I've come to expect from these two.

There's something different this time though. The red-head seems to really like this new guy, much more so than any of the dance partners in the last 6 nights that I've been watching them. As for me, I'm sat in a corner watching them, just waiting for the right moment to move in, and I have a feeling that it's almost time.

The red-head is sat in a booth and is really getting it on with the lucky guy now. From my vantage point I can see the seduction going into overdrive, some crotch-grabbing action, a lot of French-kissing, and then the red-head is pulling him up, dragging him towards the toilets. I look around for the blonde but have no luck. I'm not sure if that's a good or a bad sign, but am starting to think this could be the moment I've been waiting for.

I sit there for a few more moments, looking for the blonde, and watching the toilet door to see if the red-head reappears. I'm just biding my time as I feel the familiar sense of excitement beginning to build within me, and am pretty much convinced that my moment is here.

By now the red-head has led the guy into the toilets, and they were all over each other as they went through the door. No prizes for guessing what they're planning on doing in there either. I give it another minute or so, gaze alternating between the loo while still scanning the club for the still missing blonde.

Still no sign though, and now I'm convinced that it's the right time. I get up, ready to make my move, noticing as I stand that my palms are feeling really sweaty now and my heart is racing. I walk towards the toilet door feeling a familiar sense of apprehension. This is what I've been waiting for, and I'm determined not to mess it up.

When I reach the toilet door I pause for breath, then put my hand on the door. I make a final check to ensure that I have everything where it should be, then push the door open and walk into the toilet.

It's already a mess in there, with blood everywhere. The red-head has forced the guy to his knees and is repeatedly punching him in the face, screaming obscenities at him.

"Fucking faggot. Take that you fucking dirty puff. You're not fucking natural you. None of your type are natural. You fucking gay wanker."

Each phrase is followed by another punch. The guys nose is broken already and I can see a few of his teeth on the floor. One of his eyes is swollen shut. But it's in serious danger of getting much worse. The blonde is stood behind the poor guy and kicking him in the back repeatedly, and as I walk through the door I hear the unmistakable sound of a rib cracking.

All of this I take in as soon as I walk through the door. Most of it I was expecting, although it's further along than I would have liked. I shouldn't have waited those last couple of minutes, should have gotten in here sooner. Which means some of the damage this poor guy has taken is my fault.

I cough to make my presence known. The other three people in the room look at me, two of them in shock, one in hope. I can sense a different kind of fear in the room now. These two scumbags don't like the fact that I've disturbed their little game. I've caught them red-handed, and they know it, and this makes them worried. As for me, it makes me smile.

I smile at the whole group, but don't say a word to them. Not just yet anyway. I can almost hear them thinking to themselves, trying to work out what I want. I see the two of them look at each other, and I know right away that they're wondering if I'm like them. Maybe I just want to join in and take a turn at kicking fuck out of the queer bastard with them.

I can sense the moment that they begin to hope, begin to think that maybe things will be okay for them after all. I know the exact split second they start to think that I'm on their side, and start to believe that they'll be able to walk away from this without any problems.

And that's the moment that I was waiting for. It's not just the taking, that's the easy part. It's the total crushing of the spirit, the look of absolute despair that I know will be on their faces in a few more seconds.

That's what I do this job for; a chance to break them totally.

I give a friendly nod to the red-head first, then another one to the blonde. I'm still smiling at them both, smiles they're starting to reciprocate, when I draw my gun and my badge and say the words they were probably least expecting, and certainly least hoping, to hear tonight.

"Kevin O'Driscoll, Stephen Tompkins. I'm arresting you both on suspicion of murder, attempted murder, battery, criminal damage, and the unlawful possession of several controlled substances that I'm pretty certain you have about your persons."

I'm actually a cop, and have been after these 2 psycho's for months, ever since we found
the first body in fact. It took us a while, but we finally came up with some suspects, but no hard evidence. So all we could do was follow them and wait for the next time.

Then the troops come in. I get one of the junior guys to read them their rights. These two guys are scum, queer bashers, with a trail of dead and broken bodies left behind them. But it no longer matters. They crossed my path, and ended up with me on their trail. The end result is always the same.

TAKEN

The Chair

It's just a chair,

nothing special.

A chair, like you

might find around a

dining room table.

An old chair.

legs scratched, probably cats.

Seat worn, pattern faded.

Just a chair, nothing special.

It lies there

in the middle of the floor,

on its side.

Above the chair

your legs still twitch

as, with your final breath,

you suddenly realise

that;

you want to live.

Too late.

The Cavalier

Toby looked around the room and thought back to all the memories that he had of this place. Losing his virginity, seeing his first child in her cot beside the bed, and the horror of the night he found she wasn't breathing.

The twins running in on Christmas mornings, insisting on everyone getting up and opening the presents, even though it was only 7am and he'd been downstairs in the pub until a couple of hours earlier with some of the regulars.

The late night phone call from Denise, his daughter, telling him that she'd landed safely in Australia with her new husband, and that at the moment she was never likely to come back. The rows and arguments over money with his wife, who had always wanted him to invest properly to save for their future, while he just wanted to lead the playboy lifestyle he felt his hard work deserved.

He walked over to the side of the bed and glanced down at Alison, his wife of thirty-seven years. She was bound to be upset when she woke up and found him gone, but Toby knew that this was one decision he wasn't able to make himself any more. It was out of his hands now, and he regretted that he couldn't say goodbye. At least he was leaving enough money behind him to ensure that she would be comfortable for the rest of her life though.

He was also pretty confident that all the regulars in the pub would help look after her. Especially Old Tom, who had always secretly had a soft spot for Alison anyway. He'd make sure she was okay and that nothing bad happened to her.

Walking to the top of the stairs, Toby was careful not to make any noise, although he suspected that this was no longer important. All those years of early morning toilet trips whilst trying to avoid disturbing Alison, a notoriously light sleeper, had instilled in him an instinct to avoid the floorboards most likely to make noise.

There was no pause at the top of the stairs; he just went straight down and into the main room of the pub. Toby had lived in The Cavalier his whole life, taking it over from his father when he had died suddenly aged just 58. His mother had followed just a few months later, unable to cope without her husband.

Now, after 60 years in the pub as man and boy, Toby was preparing to leave the place behind. He stood by the bar and thought back to all the things he'd seen in his time here. The fights, the singsongs, the advent of Karaoke, (short lived in his pub as the regulars couldn't stand it).

Sky coming along and dominating sports coverage, people putting up big screens to encourage the football fans to come in, little realising that football plus alcohol could so often equal violence, which would then mean a hefty bill for putting the place back together again. Usually just in time for the next football related riot.

Some people just never learned from their mistakes.

He thought of all the people he'd seen come and go over the years from his perch at the end of the bar, and the way the pub had constantly had to adjust to the changing times in order to remain viable as a business, especially in the last twenty years with the decline of the Dockyard.

He didn't bother turning on the lights as he made his way towards the front door. After all these years he knew where every table and chair was positioned, and was never in any danger of banging into the furniture. He paused briefly at the doorway, thinking about how many times over the years he had opened this door to customers.

Stepping outside into the cool morning air, he stood at the top of the steps and looked around him at the view one last time. This was it, he knew. There was no going back now.

He stood there for several minutes, trying to work up the courage to finally walk away from the only home he had ever known. Even as he stood there on the steps he could sense the moment Alison awoke, and knew it was only a matter of moments before she realised he was gone.

Finally, as the first sounds of Alison crying began to be heard, the spirit of Toby walked down the steps of the Cavalier and left Chatham Dockyard – it was for good this time.

Bomb Damaged Lager

It's 6am, and the city is slowly starting to wake up. Today is going to be remembered for many years to come, but not for the reasons people right now are expecting to remember it for.

The date is Saturday, June 15th, 1996, and later today Italy are going to play Germany in a European Championship Football match at Old Trafford, about 4 miles down the road from where I currently sit.

Also today, England will play Scotland at Wembley, another European Championship match. Right now, I haven't decided where I'm going to go to watch the England game, although chances are it will be right where I am now, downstairs in the pub. But for now I have more pressing things on my mind. I think it's time I went to bed.

I'm more than a little bit drunk right now because I've been drinking with my new friends from the Czech Republic all night. They've come over here for the football and can't speak English, and I don't speak a single word of Czech. It's no big problem though as we all speak fluent Drunkenese.

By 10am shoppers are pouring into Manchester City Centre. Tomorrow is Fathers Day, so of course lots of kids are in town looking for presents with their mothers. Add in all the Czechs, Germans and Italians that are here for football, and we already have an estimated 70,000 people in the Arndale Centre, Manchester's main shopping arcade.

It's a beautiful day, the sun is shining, and it's already looking like being a record breaker in the shops. Me? I'm still sleeping, but I have an excuse as I was still drinking a couple of hours ago. And with Czech people no less. Man can those guys put it away! Anyway...

At about this time the coded warnings are starting to come in. Apparently, there's a bomb in Manchester City Centre, and it's a big one. Oh, and by the way, it's going to go off in about an hour. What do you mean can we tell you where it is? Don't be silly. If you want it, you'll have to look for it. Happy hunting.

Thirty minutes later the Police have pulled out all the stops and actually found the bomb. All we need now is the bomb disposal guys to turn up and defuse the damn thing. Me? Still asleep I'm afraid. I'm even managing to sleep through the Police helicopter hovering over the city telling people to get the hell away from the Arndale Centre in 5 different languages.

At 11am the bomb disposal experts arrive and get straight to work on defusing the bomb, which could take a little time. Meanwhile, the Police are working on pushing 70,000+ people out of the Arndale Centre and behind a secure cordon.

By 11.20 the bomb disposal guys are ready to do a controlled explosion, and all they're waiting for now is the Police to tell them the area is clear, just in case there's a mistake. They never get the all clear though, and the bomb goes off. 3000 pounds of explosives, packed into the back of a truck, and parked outside a shopping centre the day before Fathers Day. It makes one hell of a bang.

In fact, the shockwave lifts me out of my bed half a mile away and flings me across the bedroom, and I wake up at an approximate height of five feet off the ground, in a horizontal position, and heading towards my bedroom wall head first at a fair rate of knots. And yes, it did hurt. A lot.

I get dressed hurriedly and run downstairs into the bar my mum owns. The only people there are my mum and my evil step-dad, and they're discussing this enormous bang between themselves, trying to work out what the hell it was. The bar has only just opened so there are no customers yet. But I'll never forget the first customer of the day.

It's a young girl. If she's 18, she's only just 18. She's wearing a uniform, and clearly works in Boot's at the bottom of the street. She's shaking like hell, crying, and is very upset, and when she asks for a glass of water my mother looks at her and asks if she's sure water is all she wants.

The girl replies that she left her purse at work when she was evacuated by the police about 20 minutes ago. Just a precaution, they said, so no need to go to the back office for any personal belongings. My mum puts a pint of lager on the bar along with a shot of brandy, and tells the girl it'll help calm her down a little.

She looks at my mother and reminds her she has no money, and is told in no uncertain terms to drink it anyway and worry about money later. And wisely does as she's told. Over the next few minutes we get her story: The police came into the store and ordered everyone to leave, and a couple of minutes later there was a huge bomb blast.

She was blown halfway across the gardens that she was stood in by the shockwave, which was why she was so upset. But by the time she left about half an hour later, in a taxi that my mother paid for, she was a little more calm.

Over the course of the next 40 minutes or so the pub was doing a roaring trade. To look at anyway. Most of the people in there didn't have any money though, and we were handing out free drinks to anyone that asked. Maybe we were a little naive, but I prefer to think we were helping people out of a tight spot.

It wasn't for long anyway. The police soon arrived and ordered everyone out of the building. It seemed like there was a possibility of more bombs so they were moving the cordon back. Only to the end of the street, maybe 100 yards or so, but it was far enough. We were being evacuated from our home.

And we weren't given time to collect any belongings either, so we left with only the money I had in my wallet to go around between me, my mum, and my evil step-dad. Fortunately though I had a fair bit, as I'd only just been paid the day before, so I figured I should have enough to last for the few hours that we wouldn't be able to get back.

Except our friends from the pub across the road just got kicked out too, and they, like us, didn't have time to get any money for themselves. So now my wallet has to keep five of us entertained. Still, it's only going to be a few hours I probably, so there's no real problem.

Shit. The girl that works in the pub and lives in the flat up the road looks like she just got evicted as well. And I know she hasn't got any money because she went home early last night. Damn. This does not look good for my wallet. Not good at all.

Then I notice the Police uniforms. These guys aren't even from Manchester - they're from Merseyside, Cheshire, West Yorkshire. Fuck me, it looks like we've got the entire North West of England police force to ourselves! So, like, what are OUR coppers doing?

They're doing the same as these guys of course - trying to clear the city centre and get people out of the way, just in case there really is another device somewhere.

The barriers go up at the top of the street. The pub, our home, is visible from where we stand, but we're not allowed to go back. How long will it be until we can go home? We ask. Nobody knows. Once the city has been searched and cleared. It's a big city.

There are now seven people in our group – myself, my mother, my evil step-dad, Maggie and Audrey from the pub across the road from us, and George, the girl who works in our pub, with her boyfriend Justin. We have a brief discussion, and then for want of anything better to do we take my wallet to the nearest pub. The time now is 12-30pm.

AT 3pm, the England-Scotland football match kicks off. By now my wallet is practically empty, and our little group is getting worried. The latest news from the cops is that we wont be getting into our home any time soon. This is not good, really not good. And then, just as the game starts, repayment for the kindness we showed the waifs and strays earlier arrives.

The landlord of the pub we're in overhears us talking, discussing what we can try to do to get some money, as although we're right on the edge of town all the ATM's are on the other side of the police cordon. He knows us all of course, as we're all in the same pool league, and so he comes up to my mother and hands her a small plastic bag, then does the same with Maggie. There's £100 in each bag, and we all look at him, bemused.

"You guys have already spent £60 in here in the last 3 hours. I know you're having problems getting access to your money right now, but hopefully this will get you through until you can get back into the pubs. If not, just give me a shout and I'll give you some more. It's not like I don't know where you live after all!"

So we settle down to watch the football, secure in the knowledge that for now, at least, we don't have to worry about anything.

By the time the game ends at 5pm we're all getting annoyed. All we want to do is go home, but the police still don't know how long we'll have to wait. We go to a different pub, just for a change. At 7pm, and with the place absolutely heaving with customers, the landlord of this pub announces that he's about to close.

Apparently he only has one barrel of beer left and he wants to save it for his regular customers tomorrow. Businessman of the year is not an award he's ever likely to win!

We wander up and down the road for the next several hours, and by the time the pubs close at 11pm there's only £30 left of the £200 we were loaned earlier. And the frightening thing is, every single one of us is stone cold sober still. We can hear periodic explosions taking place throughout the city, as the police detonate every suspect package they find on site, and bearing in mind that it's a Saturday, and that everyone has had to leave town in a hurry, there's a lot of things lying around. Even handbags are being blown up.

At 1am we go up to the barrier and ask the police officer on guard duty there if there's any possibility we can be allowed to go home. We speak to him politely and respectfully, despite our tiredness, as this is the same guy that came and asked us to leave the pub well over 12 hours ago. He's been stood here ever since, and he's got to be even more pissed off at things than we are.

He gets on his radio and asks a question, then tells us that we need to go to the other side of town where they've set up a mobile command post to get passes. Ordinarily, this would be a ten minute walk, but with the cordon around the city, a cordon we are not allowed to breach without passes, we're looking at a four mile walk at least. It's decided that myself, my mother, and Maggie will go.

So we walk. And we walk. And then we walk some more. The city is desolate, no people around except cops on every corner, protecting the outside of the cordon for all they're worth. As we walk we talk about what a long day we've had, and how we can't wait to get home. And all the time there are small explosions going on all around us.

We get to the point where the cordon has been moved in, and clearly this part of town has been checked and cleared of devices. As we pass another street corner, a cop with a strange accent calls out to us.

"Excuse me, do you guys know where the Palace Theatre is. Apparently we've just received a call of another bomb threat there." His discipline is lax, and clearly he's tired. He must be tired obviously, or he'd have some idea about where he was stood.

"See that building you're leaning against there mate," I ask him casually.

"What about it?"

"Did you not notice the red neon sign right above your head, which I guess you could have missed as it's turned off? The one that says 'Palace Theatre' on it?"

He looks up, sees for himself that I am speaking the truth, and turns a very strange and pale shade, then walks away from the building as he mutters into his radio. We continue on our journey.

It takes another 20 minutes or so, but at about 2-15am we arrive at the mobile command post. It appears they've been kept informed of our progress around the perimeter, because as soon as we arrive an officer steps out with some passes in his hand.

"These will get you through the cordon at the top of Oldham Street. You understand of course that once in you will not be allowed to leave the premises for any reason without reporting to the officer on duty at that cordon to explain your movements and get permission."

With that short speech over he thrusts the passes at us and wanders back inside. We look at each other and shrug, there's nothing else for it. We begin the long walk back around town.

At just after 3-30am we finally get back to where the others have been waiting for us all this time. We explain the conditions to them and show our passes to the same copper that's been stood there all this time. And then, finally, we go home.

Five minutes later I make my way back up the street with a cup of coffee and a meat and potato pie that I'd just nuked in the microwave. It was the least we could do for the poor cop that had been stood on the street corner all day and night.

It would be Wednesday evening before our street was finally re-opened, and in the meantime we had to deal with the idiocy of having to walk to the top of our street to get permission to walk to the pub directly across the street from us in order to speak to our friends. And of course, do the same again when we wanted to return. We did have one customer that seemed to be able to slip in and out of the cordon with impunity, but we never found out how he was managing that.

When the street was finally re-opened at 6pm on Wednesday evening, we sat outside the bar with a group of our friends. As people slowly started making their way down the street, returning to the shops and offices they'd deserted in such a rush five days previously, one of our group suddenly started shouting to all and sundry.

"Bomb damaged lager. Get your bomb damaged lager. Only full price. Special offer today. Bomb damaged lager. Come and get it folks."

Trust

Should I be glad my sister is no longer here? Usually, I'd answer 'no' to that question for sure, but this isn't really a usual situation. I've not spoken to my sister for many years, and all because she wouldn't admit she had a problem.

Am I glad she isn't here any more? Not really. I wish I'd spent more time trying to convince her to get the help she needed, and then maybe, just maybe, she'd still be here. As it is, I'll never get the chance to find out why she did it.

It started when we were both nine years old. We were sisters, of course, and as we only had a small house we shared a room together. We'd always shared a room anyway as we were twins, so I guess you could say that even when we were in the womb we were sharing a room.

Anyway, when we were nine years old, my sister started climbing into bed with me occasionally. She didn't feel comfortable on her own, she'd say, or was scared of the dark, or something. There was always a new reason. So we'd share a bed for the night, and being kids we'd sometimes fall asleep in each others arms after a long cuddle.

So it all started innocently enough, but gradually things started to become less innocent. My sister would touch me in places I hadn't been touched before, or even thought of touching myself either. She'd take my hand and use it to touch herself in the same places.

Gradually I realised that she was getting some sort of pleasure out of this, but I couldn't understand any of it. Why was she doing it? What pleasure could she possibly be getting out of it? Where had she learned that by touching yourself in a certain way you could have feelings like the ones she was clearly experiencing?

I didn't understand any of it, and I certainly didn't want to take part in any of it. But we were close in that way that only twins can be close, and I didn't want to do or say anything to her that might jeapordise that closeness, so I went ahead with whatever she wanted. What else was a nine year old girl to do?

The abuse lasted for over three years, by which time we were both twelve years old, and then she discovered boys and started to leave me alone. Physically anyway, or at least most of the time.

She'd still come up behind me when I was least expecting it and grab me in places that can only be described as personal. She'd whisper all of her latest fantasies in my ear, and regale in telling me what she'd like to do to me if she got the chance.

I remember my first boyfriend, and how my sister wanted us to have a threesome together. The fact that she mentioned it to him, and he was clearly up for the idea in a big way, was one of the main reasons we split up. Me and him I mean - she was always there in the background somewhere.

From the time I was about fourteen I started asking her to go and get help, but she wouldn't listen. She would just stand there and tell me what we'd done a few years earlier was totally natural, all part of growing up, which of course I knew was patently untrue by now.

At other times she'd either deny anything had ever happened, clearly I had a vivid imagination or something, or tell me how it was all my fault. She'd only done those things because I made her do them. I could never understand either argument though, as I couldn't think of anything I may have done to cause her to behave the way she did, and I certainly knew it wasn't all just a figment of my imagination.

The hard part was, she was so sincere when she said these things that part of me started to believe it myself. Maybe if I'd protested a little more in the beginning she would never have progressed to the next level, so maybe it really was all my fault after all.

My fault in the fact that I let her do those things and never asked her to stop.

Did that mean that I was the one with a problem? I didn't think so. Surely the fact that it was her that instigated the whole thing, her that kept on escalating things that little bit further, and her that had all the new ideas for things to do and to try, meant that she had a problem. And a much bigger problem than any I might have if she couldn't even admit to doing these things.

The older I got, every guy I got involved with, she'd be there, hanging over my shoulder and flirting with him, trying to drive a wedge between me and whoever I was seeing at the time. Twice I caught her with boyfriends of mine in what the tabloid newspapers would call 'compromising positions'.

Needless to say, on both occasions they didn't stay boyfriends for long.

And what got me both times was the look on her face when I caught her. She looked happy, delirious almost, like she WANTED me to catch them. She just didn't seem to realise that what she was doing was wrong. She even came up to me once and said that she was doing me a favour by coming on to my boyfriends.

Better that I find out now, she said, that they were the unfaithful kind than in a few years when I had kids crawling around biting my ankles and stuff. And the scary part of that was that in a way she was right. But did she have to take so much pleasure out of it?

The turning point in our relationship came when I went to college. Finally I was away from her influence, and I could see who I wanted, do whatever I liked, and not worry about my sister lurking around somewhere in the background, looking for a chance to spoil things for me.

I met a nice guy while I was in college, and we got talking, and before long we found that we shared many common interests. It took a long time, but eventually I opened up to him about my past, even though it was in a drunken row when he asked me one time too many why I was so reluctant to take him home to meet my family.

I was expecting ridicule from him maybe, or some sort of leering expression like guys always seem to get when they think of two girls getting it on together, but the way he reacted showed me that he was the one for me, the guy of my dreams.

He took me in his arms, started to kiss my tears from my face, and told me that he would never mention my family again unless I raised the subject myself. He also talked me into going to see a therapist, who explained that all my doubts and insecurities were normal. And that my sisters behaviour was not.

Before long we were married, and what a wonderful marriage it turned out to be. Nine years on and we have kids of our own. We row occasionally, as all couples do, but we're happy together and I see no reason for that to ever change. I truly did find a wonderful man for myself, for which I will always be grateful.

I'm writing this though because I received a letter today. As I sat at the funeral my mother came up to me and handed me a plain white envelope with my name on it. It had apparently been found at the side of my sisters body, and I was assured that it hadn't been opened by anyone.

When I read the letter I cried for nearly two hours. My sister finally apologised to me for the things she did when we were children. She told me how she'd loved me in a way that deep down she knew was wrong, and that she hadn't been able to accept herself that she was feeling the way she was. Or the things she was feeling for me.

So she'd tried to keep those feelings hidden, and for the most part succeeded as the years went by. She told me in her final letter how she was glad that I'd found someone that could make me happy, yet at the same time it had torn her apart to see me so happy with someone other than her. It had torn her apart so much, in fact, that she'd been unable to cope and had finally given up the will to live.

Don't get me wrong, she didn't kill herself, if that's what you're thinking. Not as such anyway. She just decided not to go and see a doctor when the pain started. For three years she battled with cancer, yet no one knew a thing about it.

When I say three years, that's just a guess of course. She wasn't diagnosed with anything until after she'd died, but three years is apparently how long it takes to die of the kind of cancer she had. Well, three years if you fight it all the way of course, so it might actually have just been a few months.

It doesn't matter much either way though. She had cancer, and no-one knew. And she didn't fight it because she didn't care if she lived or died. So yes, I'm sorry she's gone. I wish she could have stood up and admitted she had a problem earlier, so it could be treated.

But I guess she just wasn't built that way. From abusing me to the cancer that killed her, she could never admit she had a problem until it was too late. My sister was stubborn right up until the very end.

As I sit here writing this I can hear my own three children playing in the yard, and as the tears flow down my face, I'm thankful that we're at least well enough off that none of them will ever have to share a room.

Ode to Frog

I wondered lonely, I'm a frog

Before I knew, I'd found the bog

The place was smelly and full of noise

Like kids in nappies, playing with toys

And then, of a sudden, I heard a cry

"Does 28 come with flied lice?"

I started to panic, and searched for escape

Before I was found, and put on a plate

I like my legs, they're rather clever

I'd hate to see them, served with pepper

Just when I thought I was going to survive

There stood a Frenchman, with a knife

He tried to grab me by the legs

And got a handful of frogsh*t instead

Addiction

Its cold, really cold.

I've been stood out here for nearly 3 hours now without even coming close to having any luck. The rain doesn't help things very much either - bad weather is never good for business.

But I persevere, as I have no real option. If I don't work I don't have any money. And, just like in all walks of life, it's money that keeps my head above water, even if it's only just above water most of the time.

I wish I knew how I'd gotten into this situation. Actually, I know exactly how I ended up here. The same way everyone else doing my job got here, through stupidity. Downright stupidity even.

There are people that knew me when I was at university that will tell you how smart I was, and how everyone knew I was going to be the one that was successful when we all finally ventured out into the real world, and for a while I was.

I was very successful, in fact. I got a great job in a respected law firm, was learning the ropes quickly, and had already been earmarked for early promotion within the first couple of years, and then I met my wife. Although she wasn't my wife then of course!

It was a staff party, thrown to celebrate some piece of shit being sent to jail for the rest of his life after beating a pensioner to death for the few quid she had left of her life savings. It had taken the jury less than 20 minutes to come back with a verdict, and there were a lot of people thinking they'd be able to sleep a lot safer once he was locked up.

So, everyone was at the party and in she walked. From where I was stood she was the most amazing looking creature on the planet. 5ft 10 or so, shoulder length brown hair, blue eyes, and a figure to die for, and the fact she was wearing the kind of dress that should be outlawed for breach of several indecency laws could have worked against her, but she had the attitude to get away with it.

I could tell just by looking at her that she wasn't some stupid bimbo slut looking for a good time, which was a shame as I could have had a really good time with her given a chance. But I knew she was out of my league right away, so I just stared at her for a couple of minutes before shaking my head and getting on with the rest of my life.

So you can probably guess how shocked I was about 20 minutes later when she came up and started talking to me. If I'd thought she was gorgeous from the other side of the room, it was nothing compared to what I thought when I was stood next to her.

I could sense all the eyes in the room were on me for the rest of the night as the two of us sat there talking and getting to know one another, and again just 3 months later when we got married. And everyone knew this was one of those relationships that was destined to go all the way.

Our first child arrived within 12 months of us getting married, and there were a couple more over the next five years. Plus I'd been promoted to junior partner at work by then, so my life was perfect. I couldn't imagine it getting much better, but I had no idea of how bad it was about to become.

It started with our youngest having an accident at school. Nothing serious really, just a clash of heads with another kid as they both went for the same ball playing soccer. He had a minor cut which was treated at hospital, but, like I said, nothing serious.

Or so we all thought. He died that night, apparently from a huge blood clot that had formed on his brain, a blood clot that the doctors said afterwards must have been growing for some time. They figured the bang on the head was the final straw. He was 7 years old.

At this point my wife fell apart. I'd like to tell you how strong I was for her, how I sat up with her night after night telling her it would get better, how I held her when she was hysterical, and made sure she didn't hurt herself when she went into a rage and started throwing things all over the place.

I'd like to tell you all that, but unfortunately, I can't. You see, I was worse than she was. Not on the outside, everyone was always commenting on how well I was coping with everything and how strong I was. But I knew the truth.

The only thing keeping me sane back then was the Columbian Marching Powder. At least, I thought it was keeping me sane, and it never occurred to me for a second that it might actually be taking over my life.

Things got worse when my wife left me. I don't blame her for leaving me, not for a minute, because she needed me and I wasn't there for her, and she lost it completely when she found out about the drugs. That was when she walked out and took our 2 daughters with her.

The drug use was getting out of control by then and was even starting to affect my work. Not in any big ways, but little lapses that could be the difference between a conviction or some scumbag walking if the other side ever picked up on them.

It all came to a head when I was called into a meeting one day about a big case. This was also the day that I went into a meeting with a very well known, very influential figure with white powder still showing under my nostrils where I hadn't wiped them properly, and the day that I cost the company a contract worth millions.

I was sacked a few days later.

In the space of less than six months I went from happily married, with 3 kids I adored and a job I loved, to homeless, jobless, and family-less. I'm pretty certain 'family-less' is a made up word in fairness, but this is my biography so if I want to use a word I've just invented then nobody can stop me.

Anyway, today is the 1st anniversary of the day I lost my job. I'm still keeping my head above water, just about sorta kinda anyway. Most days I earn enough money to get me through the day, a on the days that I dont there's a couple of people who will help me out a little if I'm really pushed. And of course, I help them out as well when I can.

Hang on a second, I think I have a customer. I'll be back in a few minutes...

...

...sorry about that. It was a customer. First one all night, but I got a good tip so I can go and get myself sorted now.

I hate my job, I really do. But when your homeless and have a drug habit, there aren't too many options open to you. So I took the only one really available - I'm a rent boy, and these days I spend most of my spare time trying to get the taste out of my mouth. For some reason everyone prefers you to swallow rather than spit, which I hate, but if I agree to it, and of course agree not to use a condom, the price goes up.

So I only usually have to do a couple a day and I have enough cash to sort myself out with whatever drugs I need to get me through the night, plus the drugs that I need so I can try and shut myself off whilst I'm actually on the job of course. But I guess I won't be doing this for much longer now.

I got a letter today, the first one I've had for a while. My test results came back, and I have AIDS, and because I can't afford the treatment I'm not expected to last much longer. I guess sharing a needle with my friends wasn't so smart after all. Or maybe it was a punter. That'd be the ultimate irony, wouldn't it? Being condemned to death because I agreed to swallow for an extra ten quid.

And everyone always thought I was the smart one! Well I guess I showed them!

One Good Cigarette

It was certainly a novel way to try and pick up women, and perhaps that was why it always seemed to work so well. Maybe just the originality of the whole thing was the secret to its continuous success.

Tim Jacobson didn't smoke. He had never smoked, and he had no intention whatsoever of even considering starting to smoke. Yet, for some reason known only to him, he never went out in public unless he had a cigarette tucked behind his ear. The brand didn't seem to matter all that much, although he did seem to have a little more luck with the low tar ones for some reason.

Actually, the truth is, Tim couldn't really remember himself why he'd started doing it. But over the years it had gotten him women, plenty of women. So he continued with it, even though all his friends were constantly giving him shit over it to begin with.

Maybe the fact he kept a lighter in his jeans pocket, so he could light the cigarette if he ever actually decided to smoke the damn thing - perhaps that was a part of the reason he was so lucky with the ladies.

If any of us ever asked him why he went everywhere with a cigarette behind his ear, his answer was always the same.

"I'm saving it for later."

"But you don't even smoke!"

"It doesn't matter. I may need it later."

That was all we ever got out of him on the subject. Weird as hell, but he did seem to be a lot luckier than the rest of us where the women were concerned. Plus, he didn't appear to mind us picking up his scraps, so to speak. And there were always plenty of scraps to pick up around him, so we all just kind of left him to whatever weird shit was going on in his own little world.

I'd known Tim for nearly three years before I finally found out the secret of the cigarette. When the privileged information was finally revealed I kicked myself mentally a few times. It was so bloody simple that I couldn't believe none of us had managed to figure it out for ourselves.

The night that Tim finally told me the method behind his madness began just like any other Friday. The guys all met up in one of the local pubs, sank a few pints, and then headed off to the local meat market. Or the nightclub, as its owners preferred it to be referred to.

Within an hour Tim had three girls hanging off his every word. No change there then. No-one knew how he did it, but we were all sure that damn cigarette had something to do with it.

I was designated to drive that night, so after two beers in the pub I'd switched to the non-alcoholic stuff. I hated soft drinks, not least because I wasn't the most self-confident guy in the world, and as a result knew I'd never stand a chance with any women sober. Mainly because I wouldn't even have the guts to even speak to them.

So, anyway, Tim had his three girls, and most of the other guys were cutting it up pretty big on the dance floor, trying to impress the ladies. And I was stood there nursing a coke and feeling pretty miserable.

It was about an hour later when Tim came up to me and pointed to a girl at the other side of the dance floor. Not just any girl either, but the most beautiful girl I'd ever laid my eyes on. And Tim said she'd been staring at me for the past 20 minutes.

I could tell just by looking at her she was way out of my league. She might think I looked okay from about 40 yards away in a dark club, but I knew if I got up close she'd just start laughing at me. And not because I was telling her really funny jokes either, which I reminded myself I could do with learning a few of, just in case they came in handy at a future date.

I explained this to Tim, and he just started laughing at me. Then he asked me what my problem was. Not only was I getting checked out, but I was getting checked out by the hottest girl in the place. And I was acting like I wasn't interested.

"It's not that I'm not interested," I shouted over the sound of the pounding music. "I am interested. Totally. But I know that as soon as she gets a close look at me she's going to go and find herself some handsome young stud to charm the pants off her, probably literally, while I'm stood there looking like a prize muppet for daring to think she'd ever even think about a guy like me."

Did I mention I was in a really bad, non-alcoholic, low self-esteem moment?

"Okay," said Tim, with a strange look on his face. "Desperate times call for desperate measures. It's time for you to learn the secret of the cigarette."

With that, he took the cigarette, (which I believe was a Marlboro Light), from behind his ear and placed it behind mine. Then he reached into his pocket, coming out with his lighter in his hand, which he also passed over to me.

"Okay dumbass. All you have to do is go over there and get talking to her. Say hello, ask her if she wants a drink. Whatever. The important thing is that you keep her talking until she asks about the cigarette."

"And if she doesn't ask about it?"

"They ALWAYS ask about it. And they usually ask sooner rather than later. Trust me on this, okay?"

"So what do I tell her when she asks? That I'm saving it for later?"

"No you idiot. You say what I always say when I know none of you guys are around to hear me."

Then he leaned towards me and whispered something into my ear. The second part of which was something along the lines of "And if you ever tell the other guys this I'll kill you." It was the first part that caused me to look at him though, searching for a sign in his eyes that there was some sort of elaborate hoax going on at my expense.

"Get your stupid fat arse over there before she gets fed up of waiting and really does go and find herself a handsome young stud, one who might not be so bloody dumb!"

And with that, he pushed me towards the dance floor. I looked back once, still convinced there was some sort of trick being played here, then turned round and walked across towards the Goddess I'd already decided somewhere in the back of my mind was the woman I was going to spend the rest of my life with. If she'd talk to me that was, so in reality it was never going to happen.

With each step I took my feet became heavier, my palms more slick with sweat. I could feel the perspiration on my face as well, running down my cheeks in what seemed like small rivers. I paused briefly to wipe a huge drop of the dreaded salty liquid from the tip of my nose, before continuing my trek across the room.

By the time I was at her side I was a wreck. I knew my face would be bright red, and that all the blotches and spots would be standing out like beacons saying "Look at me. Imperfect Skin! Imperfect Skin!" My heart was pounding, shirt plastered to my back by now. I was a mess, and I knew I was a mess.

But somehow, from somewhere, I plucked up the courage to speak to her.

"Excuse me. Can I buy you a drink?"

Okay, not the most original chat-up line a guy ever attempted. In the circumstances though, the fact I managed to say anything at all was certainly a score for the good guys from where I was standing.

She turned around and looked me up and down. I knew what she was going to say before she spoke, and was already turning around and getting ready to walk off, hearing the words "fuck off jackass", or something similar, even in advance of them being spoken.

My face was bright red with embarrassment, knowing that I should have stayed where I was rather than confront this vision of perfection in front of me. I was fully turned around and starting to walk away by the time she finally spoke.

"Wait! Why have you got a cigarette behind your ear?"

I turned back to face her, gave her what I hoped was a cocky, confident grin. Then I answered with the line Tim had given me. Knowing it was stupid, that there wasn't a chance in hell it would work, but no longer caring. At that point, I was willing to say anything to prolong the conversation with her, even if only for a few more seconds.

"I'm saving it for later. In case I bump into a beautiful woman in desperate need of a smoke."

She smiled. I don't know how, but suddenly the dark club seemed to be a lot lighter than I ever remembered it being before.

"So," she asked, as she reached behind my ear and took the cigarette. "Do you have a light as well? Or am I not beautiful enough for you?"

That was eight years ago. Three months later, I asked her to marry me, and she agreed. We now have a couple of kids, and she stopped smoking when she was pregnant with our first child because she was worried about the harm it may do to him. And I never smoked anyway.

But we have an agreement. In a case just above the living room fire there is a single cigarette, just to remind us that yes, smoking kills. But every now and then, and despite all medical evidence to the contrary, occasionally cigarettes can actually be good for you.

And in case you were wondering, yes, Tim was the Best Man at our wedding.

The Lidless Eye

Given the amount of time that Brantley had been down the hole it was amazing that his single, lid-less eye could still focus at all. I was hoping that this wouldn't last much longer though as I was hungry and wanted to go home for my tea, provided my stomach would be able to take food once I got out of here of course. Still, that's more than enough about me.

Brantley was 13 years old, and I'd been looking for him for some time, ever since he'd been kidnapped in fact. There hadn't been much in the way of clues as to his whereabouts until a few days earlier, when all of a sudden his parents had received a package in a plain white envelope, with the address printed neatly on the side. And inside the envelope was a small plastic bag. It was this bag that had contained the eyelid, and DNA testing with the kid's parents had soon made it clear where the eyelid had come from.

So we'd stepped up the search. Meanwhile, his parents were waiting for an actual demand to be made. They were willing to pay whatever ransom was required, and they could well afford it. The only problem though was that so far there was no actual demand. No demand, no ransom to pay. Not good.

Things, to put it mildly, had not been going well. Then we'd got a lucky break. Analysis of the envelope gave us a fingerprint. Not a full one, but enough for us to run it through the database to see if there were any probable matches. The database wasn't as efficient as we'd have liked though. It gave us 113 matches.

So we'd had to work hard to try to eliminate them all. 52 were easy as they belonged to people who were dead already, and another 27 were currently serving time in jail. Which left us with 34, and of those 11 were small time crooks into things like stealing cars and burglary, and we figured they wouldn't have had the intelligence for a scam like this.

The last 23 we had to physically check out though, one by one, which of course took longer than anybody would have liked. In the end though, like the famous Canadian Mounties, we finally got our man. It was too late to save the boys left eye though, as that had arrived on his parents' doorstep yesterday morning.

Half an hour later we arrested Phil Jenkins, who was the caretaker of the house next door to the Brantley's and who, it turned out, had a charge sheet longer than Osama Bin Laden's would be if they ever found him. Mostly for nice things, stuff like extortion and violence.

It had taken a while for him to realise that it would go better for him if we found what was left of Brantley still in one piece. I mean, don't get me wrong, he was going to jail for the rest of his life for this one regardless, but there's jail, and then there's jail.

He could either go in and be protected, which we promised he would be if we found the boy in time, or he could go in as a child killer and have to face all the other inmates. Once he weighed up his options he came around to our way of thinking, which was fortunate for us as the kid had already been missing for eight days by now.

So that's how I come to be standing here now, knee deep in mud in the middle of nowhere at stupid o' clock in the morning. Another few minutes and we should have him out of there, and then we can all go home and congratulate ourselves on a fucking job well done.

Even if we did get lucky, and weren't really that efficient. All that really matters is the boy, and he looks like he's going to be okay. Well, except for his vision, obviously. I can't believe that the sick freak took off his right eyelid and then removed his left eye. The poor kid will never be able to close his eye properly ever again. Which probably explains the poor focus now I think about it.

Being Cool is Easy

Learn the phrases, learn the walk
To geeks and nerds we never talk
Fashion first, morals second
Fake I.D.s to become a legend

Always striving to impress
Spend a fortune on a dress
Perfect nails, shiny hair
Tramps want money? None to spare

Only eat at the best places
Lookout for the famous faces
Down our noses, that's the way
The only way to look at gays

Even when our greatest friend
Admits she doesn't fancy men
Best of friends, or so she reckoned
Now discarded in just seconds

Learn the phrases, learn the walk
To gays and niggers, we don't talk
Being cool is easy, being cool is false
Being cool can ruin lives,
Just like sex can give you hives

Being cool is easy, being cool is free
Being cool is easy, but I'm sorry
I'd rather be me

Donors

"Good morning. Can you just fill this out for me please, then take a seat over there and I'll be with you shortly."

"Sure, no problem," I replied, taking the proffered clipboard and making my way over to the seats. I've never been here before, and to be honest, I'm a little bit nervous. It's something that I feel I should do though, and nervous as I am I'd encourage other people to do the same thing even as I sit here and start to fill in the form.

It's a simple enough form, just a load of questions with yes and no answers, and all you have to do is tick boxes. So simple that even I can manage it in the space of about 40 seconds or so, which isn't bad for about 50 questions. What do you mean I'm supposed to read the questions before ticking the boxes?

Form completed, I sit and wait for them to get round to dealing with me. I have a look around while I'm waiting, and the first thing to catch my attention is the girl just walking through the door. 5 feet 8 tall, long, straight, black hair, practically no make-up, a sweet face, and the kind of figure that has most guys jaws on the floor. Including, I'm not afraid or ashamed to admit, my own.

She approaches the desk, gets a form, and then comes and sits next to me to fill it out. Which I'm not complaining about of course, but seeing as the room is practically empty and there are at least 30 free seats, I automatically start to draw certain inferences from the fact she's chosen to sit by me.

It's a guy thing I think. Any time a good looking girl sits near you when she has no need to, you just assume that she must like the look of you and that you might actually be in with a chance with her. Of course, the fact that you're fat and ugly and haven't had a bath in a week is completely disregarded at this point, and the fantasies just set themselves off running in your head.

Or is that just me?

Anyway, before I'd even had time to start thinking of a way to break the ice and introduce myself, one of the pesky assistants, clearly with no regard for either loves young dream or timing, calls my name, and off I go into one of the little cubicles.

There follows a stream of questions that I answer automatically. How many questions exactly? I don't know. What were they about? I have no idea. My brain is in some sort of fog and all I can think about is the girl with the dark hair and the fact that she chose to sit next to me, and now I'll probably never get another chance to speak to her because some stupid cow wanted to ask me a load of silly questions.

I get asked to hold my thumb out and do so without thinking. Next thing I know there's a sharp prick and they're taking a blood sample from the end of my thumb.

"To test for iron and make sure you're not anaemic," comes the unrequested explanation.

"If there isn't enough iron in my blood I'm taking Guinness to court. I had 17 pints of the stuff last night," I reply, starting to come out of my mind funk.

"There's plenty here by the look of it, very iron rich blood. Now, if you can just take a seat outside we'll be with you in a moment."

So back out of the cubicle I go, hoping against hope that she might still be sat in the same place and that I might get a chance to speak to her this time. My hope is all in vain though unfortunately, as she's already vanished. Probably her turn for the stupid questions and the thumb prick treatment.

I wait for maybe 5 minutes, which should be more than enough time for her to be out of the cubicle, before my name is called. I wander into the next room feeling strangely sad, as it's clear by now she's gone and I've missed her, probably never to see her again. Why do I feel like this over someone I only saw for a brief moment and never spoke to? It makes no sense.

I get directed over to one of the beds, and they set about the preparation stages. Confirm name and date of birth in case I came in as a substitute for someone else in the last couple of minutes when they weren't looking or something, then up on the bed, arm out to the side, and blood pressure cuff put on. And then they walk away and leave me there.

I look around the room, still thinking about the girl I'd seen in reception, still ridiculously troubled by my reaction after such a brief encounter, and then there she is. Walking into the room, asked by the assistant which arm she wants to use, and pointing to the bed next to mine and saying "I don't mind as long as I can have that bed there."

Now it's obvious to even an idiot like me that she's deliberately making an effort to get close to me, even though I can't for the life of me work out why, and this makes me bold enough to start to speak to her as she lies down beside me.

"So, do you come here often?"

Corny as hell I know, but I have a silly grin on my face that makes it obvious that I'm not being serious. At least, I think that's what the grin on my face means. It's certainly what it's supposed to mean!

"Every now and then," comes back the reply. "I really like the ambience and the atmosphere of the place, and you hardly ever have to wait to get served."

"I agree. I always find it so annoying at those places where you have to queue for ages to get what you want."

"And what is it you want exactly?"

This last question is asked with a mischievous glint in her eyes and a smile on her face, and suddenly I start to believe that I really do have a chance with this girl, ridiculous though such a thought seems even to me.

"Sorry to interrupt you two, but can we just get things started please," says the assistant, who instantly wins the prize for most ill-timed interruption of the year, for the second time in 10 minutes. I really hate that woman with a passion, and her sticking a needle in my arm, even if this whole thing was my idea, does nothing to appease my feelings.

She finally finishes up and moves away to sort out another victim, sorry, volunteer, and I glance over to my left to the beautiful woman lying there beside me.

"You never answered my question. What do you want?"

"I guess I don't get out of it that easily then?" I say, stalling for time as I try to think of something socially acceptable to say in reply.

"No, you don't. Now stop stalling and tell me what you want." She's persistent, I'll give here that much.

"I'd like to take you out for a drink when we finish here, if that's okay."

"No, sorry, not good enough. Alcohol is not allowed and I don't really fancy going to the pub and drinking soft drinks. That just defeats the object."

"What about a meal then?"

"Better idea, because we are advised to eat. Problem is, if we go to a restaurant, I'm going to have to drink wine, and that's not allowed."

"What about a walk then? Surely there can't be anything wrong with that?"

"Of course there is. Walking is exercise, exercise is tiring, when you get tired you get thirsty, and when you get thirsty there's always a pub nearby, and then we'd be too tempted to go and drink. Bad idea."

"I don't know then. Have you got any ideas about what we can do?"

"Well we could go back to my place and make love all afternoon, and night, and maybe even tomorrow morning if you're not working."

"I can always phone in sick I suppose. I've been working there nearly a month now so I'm due a sickie."

"That's a plan then. Now all we need is to get these needles out of our arms and away we can go."

Which is exactly what we do. If I was a little shocked at how forward she was, I've never been a guy to look a gift horse in the mouth, so we finished donating blood, walked outside together, got into a taxi and went straight back to her place, where we fell straight into bed with each other and stayed there for the next three days. It cost me my job of course, as I never did get around to phoning in sick, but I reckon it was worth it.

On the morning of the fourth day, just as we were lying there trying to get the energy together to either get up and do something or just roll over and do each other again the doorbell rang. She threw on a robe and walked gingerly downstairs, clearly feeling the effects of the last couple of days, and then came back a few minutes later with a huge bouquet of flowers and a big smile on her face.

"Happy anniversary to you too darling. To think that it's ten years today since we first met giving blood."

"I know, it's crazy isn't it. And I never really believed all those adverts back then saying 'Do something amazing, give blood'. If I hadn't chosen to give blood that day though, I'd have missed out on the most amazing ten years of my life."

"Me too honey. Now I really have to get moving as I was supposed to pick the kids up two days ago!"

Consequences

The first thing I noticed as I entered the house was the silence. No matter where I stepped there was never the familiar sound of a creaky floorboard, which was strange as there were several that had always creaked before.

The second stair from the top, for example that one was guaranteed to always creak at just the slightest pressure. Yet here I was, practically jumping on it, and not a sound to be heard.

I was starting to get worried about the total lack of sound in the place when I saw my daughter come out of her room and pick up the telephone. She answered the call, and then seemed to get upset about something, but for some reason I was unable to hear what she was saying. Even when I stood right behind her, I still couldn't hear a thing.

Maybe I'd gone deaf. Yes, that could explain it. Try as I might, I couldn't come up with any other explanation as to why I couldn't seem to hear anything, except deafness of course. Deafness worked for sure as an explanation.

I noticed that my daughter was still on the telephone, and was quite clearly seriously distressed by now, so I did what any parent would do and put my arms around her. She seemed to stiffen up for a second, which I took for surprise or something, as obviously the poor girl hadn't realized that I was standing right behind her.

And yet, once the initial moment of stiffness had passed she carried on as she had been before. No acknowledgement of my presence. No reciprocated hug or anything. By now I was seriously worried, as whatever it was that had gotten her into this state was clearly something serious.

I got up, leaving my daughter crying into the phone, and went around the house, looking for my wife. Maybe she'd be able to tell me what was wrong with our eldest child. They'd always been close to each other, closer than I was to any of the kids. I was sure my wife would know what the problem was.

And then I stopped, and started to remember things. Things like what I'd been doing just before walking into the house of silence. I'd been driving, and chatting to my agent on my mobile phone.

My wife and I had gone to pick up our twin sons up from school. The holidays were starting, and in another week and it would be Christmas. There was some snow around, but not too much, nothing compared to what the weather forecasters were predicting for the weekend anyway.

So we picked the boys up, no problems there, and started driving back home, and that was when my agent called to tell me there was a problem with the new deal. It looked like it might fall through if we didn't move quickly to sort it out, so I arranged a meeting for the next morning.

I think it was probably about this time that I heard the screaming start. The screaming that seemed to be coming from Daniel, the youngest of the twins by exactly 11 minutes and 27 seconds. I turned round to him to see what the problem was, and I think that was when the train hit us.

I'm not sure what happened to be honest. I guess I must have missed the sign for the level crossing or something, and the flashing warning lights, and everything else that was put in place to stop idiots driving in front of trains, as I was too busy talking to my agent.

The screaming seemed to go on for hours, along with the sounds of rending metal, glass breaking, and the train horn practically in my ear. Then there was silence. For a long time, nothing but silence.

The next thing I recall is walking into the house, and I understood it all now. This was my chance to say goodbye. I was dead, there was no chance I could have survived that. And my wife, she was dead too, as were the twins.

Which left Sharon, 13 years old, a few days before Christmas, and now all alone. No wonder she was upset.

I looked down at myself, and noticed that I seemed to be fading away. As soon as the changes became evident, they seemed to speed up, so that in seconds I could no longer see myself.

I could still think though, and I suspect that I'll be able to think for a long time to come yet. About the life of one young girl, and the deaths of 3 people I loved dearly. People killed because I was more interested in a business call than I was in the business of driving my family home.

Hijack

The call had come in to the operations centre at 5:46pm local time. An airline was named, as was a specific flight number, and the departure and destination airports. Such threats were commonplace, and for the most part they were pretty much ignored, but this one came from a double agent who was high up in the terrorist network. The threat was real.

They had six hours to decide how to respond to the threat, and then to facilitate that response. The first call was the simplest one, cancel the flight. No flight equals no risk. It was a fairly easy equation to understand, and it wouldn't be the first time such action had been taken.

There were some who disagreed with this plan though. These were the people you read about in spy thrillers who were high up in certain shadowy organisations, and who of course wanted the plane to fly as normal so as not to risk blowing the cover of their agent. In the end, as often happens in these cases, a compromise was reached.

The plane would fly as normal but security would be extra tight, and far more vigilant than normal. The people on the ground had to be warned of the threat, as one mistake could prove fatal for over four hundred people on the plane, plus unknown and unpredictable casualties on the ground.

Tommy Malone looked around the departures hall as he prepared to check in. It could have been any airport in the world, with its banks of check in desks dedicated either to a specific airline or to a specific carrier group. As always, British Airways had a whole rank of desks just to themselves, as did a few of the big American companies, while everyone else made do with sharing.

Looking down the line in front of him, Tommy could see that security was a lot tighter than normal. Each piece of hand luggage was being inspected minutely before being passed, and dogs were sniffing around everywhere. Obviously there had been some sort of threat made against the plane, but perhaps one that wasn't being taken too seriously or the flight would have been cancelled.

Tommy was well aware of just how serious the real threat was though, and as he moved forwards he started to wonder whether the plan was as flawless as it appeared. He was sure he'd find out soon enough.

Another look around the hall and he spotted two of the others, Mike and Sue, posing as a happily married couple even though they'd only met a couple of days previously. Mike seemed to be enjoying the pretense though, and perhaps taking it a bit too far as he suddenly pulled Sue to him and started to kiss her passionately.

Then again, they'd been forced to spend most of their time together in the last few days, so maybe they'd decided to make the relationship as personal as it was supposed to be after all. The only thing they really had to worry about was the quality of the passports, although they should be okay as they'd come from one of the best in the business.

Tommy stepped forwards to the desk, his turn to check in at last. He felt himself start to sweat a little as last minute nerves started to hit him. What if the passport wasn't clean after all, or what if they realised what the canister was for? What if, what if, what if? He knew it was perfectly natural to react like that, but he had to stay calm otherwise the whole plan could be blown.

The usual boring and inane questions; "Did you pack your bag yourself sir? Has anyone else had access to your bag sir?" resulted in the usual answers, and then it was time for the question that wasn't normally asked at check in, but which everyone complied with when asked because they didn't really have a choice.

"Do you mind if I take a look inside your bag sir?"

"Not at all," replied Tommy, reaching into his pocket for the key to the padlock almost before he was asked. "I knew I shouldn't have worn my jacket to the airport. It's a bit warm today isn't it mate?" Tommy continued, trying to make polite conversation whilst suffering his bag being searched.

"You do seem to be sweating rather a lot sir," came the reply. "Why don't you squirt yourself with a bit of this to save whoever sits next to you having to put up with 14 hours of you stinking!"

With that the security officer handed Tommy the can of deodorant that was in his bag, and Tommy gratefully squirted under his armpits before casually putting the can into his jacket pocket. A few seconds later and he was walking away from the desk, the hard part of the job done. Now all he had to do was wait.

He went to the bar and ordered himself a coffee, then changed his mind and asked for a pint of lager instead. If things went according to plan this would probably be his last ever drink, and he didn't want to go and meet his maker with the smell of crappy Nescafe on his breath.

Glancing around the bar, Tommy noticed that the whole team had made it through the security checks unscathed. Six of them in all, and despite the extra security each and every one of them was carrying a potentially lethal weapon. It would be especially dangerous in the enclosed and pressurised cabin of a cruising airliner.

The flight was called and everyone started to line up to board. There was another security check as people were about to go along the ramp to the plane, and clearly the authorities were taking this threat pretty seriously, but once more the entire team walked through without question.

The fools thought they had the situation under control, thought Tommy, when in fact it was anything but. Still, he knew that they weren't sure of anything until the plane took off. Then they'd be ready to take over, and nothing would be able to stop them.

The pre-flight ritual was one Tommy had been through countless times before, and it always bored him to tears. As for the demonstrations of what to do in an emergency, that was just a waste of time. Not one of the instructions mentioned what to do in case of a hijacking, and in reality this rendered the whole practice useless.

Twenty minutes later and the plane was airborne at last, and Tommy started to psych himself up for what was to come next. First they'd have to wait for the seatbelt light to go off, as not only would they look suspicious moving before then, but also that would mean the plane was at a suitably high altitude for the cabin to be fully pressurised.

They didn't have long to wait, and then it was time to act, and as soon as the seatbelt light went off the entire team of six stood up in unison. Half of them went for the overhead lockers and their hand luggage, whilst the others made their way towards the toilets at the front and rear of the plane.

Sue was the last one to get her bag down, and as soon as she had what she wanted in her hands she shouted to her friends that it was time. As soon as she shouted, six hands went into pockets and withdrew lighters. Then six people simultaneously started to spray the cans of deodorant they had in their hands before putting the now lit lighters to the streams escaping from the nozzles.

The result? From being a perfectly normal flight, all of a sudden there were six people armed with flamethrowers on board, and everyone started to panic. Well, almost everyone started to panic. There were a few people on board though who had been ready for just such an event.

Six of the people who didn't panic held flamethrowers in their hands, and as a result considered themselves to be in control of things. The other three people who didn't panic were sat in the middle of the cabin, within a few seats of each other, and they loved this kind of situation.

The three rose in unison and reached into their jackets, withdrawing snub-nosed revolvers of a type extremely difficult to get hold of. These were not ordinary guns, as to use such a thing in a pressurised environment would only result in disaster. They were in fact gas powered and contained rubber bullets, as opposed to metal.

Numerous safety tests had been performed before they'd been deemed suitable for use on commercial airlines, and the three people holding them now were the best in the business when it came to neutralising terrorists.

Seconds later and all six would be hijackers were on the ground, and the situation was no longer out of control. The best thing about the rubber bullets, of course, was that they didn't kill the targets, and the three young men who had used them so effectively were certain that the six terrorists would soon be telling all they knew of their organisation to the interrogators.

Meanwhile, with the situation averted, it was down to the pilot to make the decision to either turn back or go on with the flight. After a brief discussion he decided to turn back to where he'd come from rather than spend upwards of twelve more hours with the terrorists on board.

Throughout the entire drama, nobody paid any attention whatsoever to the young girl in seat 27D, who, as the plane started to turn around, reached into her pocket and pressed a button to turn on her Walkman...

Flight BA793 started its approach to Manchester International Airport less than twenty minutes later. On board were six bound and gagged terrorists, and three men who described themselves as Sky Marshals, although nobody really believed them. Whoever they were though, everyone was pleased that disaster had been averted, and they were all more than happy not to ask too many questions of their saviours.

The pilot checked his altitude as he began the final approach to the runway. He never bothered to look down at Ringway Road as the plane passed over it, and if he had he probably wouldn't have realised the significance of what he saw anyway.

A lone motorcyclist sat astride his bike, which was idling at the side of the road, watching the plane as it got closer and closer. Just as the plane passed overhead he reached into his backpack and withdrew a SAM 71 rocket launcher, then quickly aimed and fired at the jet.

There was no need for anything fancy with this weapon, just point and shoot and away you go. Three seconds later the belly of the plane was torn apart by the missiles impact, and it was already in pieces by the time it landed a few seconds after that.

The motorcyclist saw none of this, as by the time the initial impact occurred he already had the bike up to 60 miles per hour as he sped away, leaving the rocket launcher in the middle of the road.

Half an hour later the bike pulled into the driveway of a farmhouse and the rider dismounted. He thought it was a shame things had worked out like they did, but that was why he was sent there as a backup. If the initial team failed, it was his job to bring down the plane, and he was being paid a lot of money to do the job.

He got himself a beer out of the fridge and sat down at the table, thinking of the friends he had lost in the last few years. Thinking, especially, about a young girl with a Walkman who had been on her first ever plane journey today. A girl with a Walkman that was not all it seemed to be, and who had used it to transmit the information that the plane was turning back.

He sat there for some time, thinking about his daughter and her sacrifice, and in the meantime people at the airport started to try and clear up the mess.

The Reaper

Just six years old, and there he lies
Alone, beside the road
The car slows down, but not for long
And then the driver goes

She's twenty-three, and full of life
Until she sees the mask
And then there's fear, and nothing more
Until she's free at last

He sits at home, awaits the call
He knows, one day will come
The call that says the words he fears
About his missing mum

She knew the risks right from the start
As she jumped from the plane
And as her 'chute fails to deploy
There's nothing she can gain

He wet the bed as a small child
Was bullied whilst at school
Until the day he'd had enough
Below him lies a stool

The nurse brings her a nice warm drink
Before she goes to bed
She knows not that it is her last
Tomorrow, she'll be dead

He boards the plane on his way home
From journeying abroad
Unknown to him the man behind
Has brought a bomb on board

She didn't know he was a cop
When she walked in the store
She needed food, she raised her gun
He blew her out the door

We live our lives, whilst all around
The tragedies unfold
Yet we go on, oblivious
Until it's one of us

And then one day we learn the truth
The truth most people fear
It matters not, your innocence
When the Reaper doth appear

Conspiracy

Why do they do it?

Why do who do what? I hear you ask. Well, I think the easiest way to explain is if I tell you a little story...

You see, today is Sunday morning, which of course means that yesterday was Saturday. And I, like single men all over the world, went out for a drink or two yesterday. No big surprise there then.

Anyway, so there I was in a club, having a few drinks, listening to the music, and doing the typical single guy thing of looking around and seeing what the female talent was like. And I can assure you, there was definitely some talent in the place last night.

And then I saw her. She wasn't just beautiful, she went beyond stunning and way out the other side. I felt my breath catch just looking at her, and then I realized that she was looking at me too.

I'd had a few drinks by this point so, bolstered up a little, I decided to be brave and chance my luck. I didn't really rate my chances, as girls who look that good have always got a guy trailing around behind them, and usually a big guy. With lots of muscles and stuff.

She was totally drop dead gorgeous though, so I figured I'd chance a beating, just in case. And it turned out she didn't have any boyfriend in tow. It was my lucky night.

So, anyway, to cut a long story short, before too much longer we'd left the club together and were on the way back to my place, where we proceeded to have lots of down and dirty fun for a few hours before falling asleep in one anothers arms.

And this is where my conspiracy theory starts.

Because when you bear in mind the stunningly attractive, drop dead gorgeous woman I had in my arms when I fell asleep, you can imagine my shock when I woke up to find a big, fat, hairy bushpig of a woman there instead.

And this is not the first time such a thing has happened.

Indeed, it's quite common for me to go to bed with total stunners and wake up with entirely the opposite.

And it's happened to some of my friends too. Quite a few times.

Which leads me to the only logical conclusion.

Women are conspiring against men to try to instill some sort of inferiority complex in our minds. And this is how they do it.

The really good looking women go trawling around the bars and clubs looking for likely candidates. Having found and decided on which lucky guy is going to be used and abused this time, they then head back to his place, or sometimes even their place, and do the deed for as long as it takes.

Right up until the guy falls asleep in fact.

They then, very quietly, get out of bed, get dressed, and call up the biggest, fattest, ugliest girl they know, give them the address, wait for them to arrive, and then swap places with them in the middle of the night.

Leaving the poor guy lay there in the morning, scratching his head and saying to himself things along the lines of...

"I know I was drunk, but I wasn't THAT drunk...was I?"

Hit and Run

I knew as soon as I woke up that it was going to be one of those days. The kind of day that you really wish you'd just turned back over and gone back to sleep when the alarm went off, even though you knew that was never really an option. It didn't help that my alarm went off so damned early that morning, piercing my head with its incessant buzzing and destroying the last vestiges of a very enjoyable dream in which I'd been on the verge of climbing into bed with two amazingly beautiful women.

What can I say? I'm a guy, it's something I dream about sometimes, and I see no reason to be ashamed about it!

Anyway, I digress. My alarm was going off, which was really annoying me, and as I sat up to check the time I became even more annoyed. It was still dark outside, which is something that always makes me cranky when I wake up, and the display on the clock confirmed what I knew already. It was only 4:30am.

I have to say that getting out of bed at that time is something that I've always had a problem with. It was even harder than usual this time though, as by my reckoning I'd actually only been in bed for ninety minutes or so. That, plus the fact that I was more than a little drunk when I finally made it upstairs, did not make me a very happy bunny. Nor did thinking about the five-hour drive I had to take shortly.

I got out of bed and did my usual three-s routine. Which is shit, shower, and shave, for those who don't understand. I felt a little healthier by then, although still not completely in touch with reality. I toyed with the idea of going across the road to the cafe to get some breakfast, then remembered that they didn't open until 6am, by which time I needed to be on the road.

As an old friend of mine would have said, that'll be breakfast skipped then.

Heading outside, I was greeted with yet another sign that today wasn't going to be a particularly nice one. It was raining. Absolutely belting down in fact. Damn! I hated driving in the rain. I especially hated driving in the rain when I was still drunk from the night before and hadn't had any breakfast.

The fact that the last place on the planet I wanted to go to was the place I was about to start driving to really did nothing to help matters. Not even 5:30am yet and it was already a shit day. On the plus side, I didn't suppose it could get much worse.

You know how sometimes you think things are as bad as they could ever possibly be, and you have the knowledge that no matter what happens, from this point on things can't possibly get any worse?

Did you ever notice that all it takes is that little piece of knowledge, that grain of whatever it is that tells you that you are now officially in the worst position it's possible to be in, to make you start to feel better?

After all, if it can't possibly get any worse, all you have to do now is start to deal with it, and before you know it things will start to improve again.

That's about how I was feeling as I set out on my long drive that morning. Of course, as is often the case with things like this, I was totally wrong. I thought my day was already as bad as it could possibly get. What I didn't realise was that moment of that particular day was actually as good as it was going to get for me for a long time.

From the moment I pulled out of the driveway and started my journey things started to go downhill, and sometimes when things start to go bad on you it happens so fast that it's over before you even realise it's started.

I swear I didn't even see the kid, and in my defence I'd ask what a kid that age was doing out at that time of the morning anyway, especially wearing just shorts and a t-shirt, in weather that was truly nasty. Maybe the weather was part of the reason I didn't see him, as visibility was down to maybe 15 feet that morning, but in the grand scheme of things it probably doesn't much matter.

I was just driving along, minding my own business as I tried to find a decent CD to keep me awake, and all of a sudden I felt the car hit something. I looked into my mirror and that's the first time I saw the kid, lying there in the middle of the road.

I think most people in those circumstances would have done the right thing and stopped, tried to make sure he was okay. And I thought about it, I really did. I thought about how I had enough alcohol in my bloodstream to get me in a lot of trouble, even if the kid had run out in front of me. I also thought about my appointment, and how important it was I get there, no matter how much I didn't want to be going there.

Having a quick look around I couldn't see anyone else, so I figured there were no witnesses. So I made the decision to continue on my journey. I had a feeling it would be easy enough to get my car fixed on my way back from where I was heading, and that way when the cops went around the local repair shops in the hope of finding the car responsible, mine wouldn't show up any red flags for them.

I should point out here and now that I did not panic. You read about hit and run accidents all the time, and it's always either the driver panicked, which is why he drove off, and these guys generally come forwards a few days later because the guilt gets to them, or the driver has reasons that he wants to avoid the police and he isn't stopping for anybody.

Well, I didn't really fall into either category. Sure, meeting the police would almost certainly cost me my licence because of what I'd had to drink the previous night. I may even get a suspended jail term. That didn't bother me though. All I was interested in was getting to where I had to go before it was too late.

So off I went, leaving the kid lying there in the rain. I didn't even stop to check how badly injured he was, as I just figured there'd be someone else along soon enough and that they'd make sure he got the treatment he needed. If he didn't, well, that would be his own fault for being out at that time of the morning. Not my problem.

I guess right now you're thinking I'm a heartless bastard, and in the circumstances I'd be inclined to agree with you. I had other things on my mind though, and whilst I'm not going to try to condone how I behaved that morning, as I don't think such a thing is possible anyway, I will try to explain why I did what I did.

After all, that is the whole point of writing this.

Anyway, about twenty minutes later I realized that I was short of fuel, so I pulled into a service station to fill up. This was to turn out to be my second mistake of the morning, although I didn't know it yet.

You see, in my part of the world petrol stations have a problem with people filling up their cars and driving off without paying occasionally, so to combat this they have a little system whereby they write down the registration of every car that pulls in. That way the police can trace you if you don't pay for your fuel.

A perfectly reasonable and understandable precaution, as I'm sure you'd agree, and also a precaution that I was well aware of, as there's no point of having such a system in place if you don't let people know about it. That's like having nuclear weapons pointed at Russia in case of attack and not telling them about it. Deterrents only work if the other side know what you have to try and deter them!

Anyway, I pulled into the station, fuelled up, and off I went to continue my journey. I guess I was too tired to notice the odd look the guy behind the counter was giving my car, or the way he moved his head back when I said good morning to him because of the alcohol on my breath.

Certainly in hindsight I should have realised he was likely to see the damage to the car, smell the booze on my breath, and then put two and two together when he heard on the radio a little while later that there'd been a hit and run in the area.

I should have realized this, but I didn't, which is why before I even knew about it my registration number was being handed out to every cop within a hundred mile radius. As I said earlier, sometimes things just start going wrong for you, and it happens so fast you don't even notice.

Anyway, about ten minutes after filling up the car I was on the motorway and heading north. My destination was 300 miles away and I had to be there by 11am. As long as there were no traffic problems though I knew I'd be able to make it there easily enough, even in this weather.

Of course, I wasn't counting on the radio telling everyone about this poor little boy who'd been left for dead in the street, or the description of my car being broadcast all over the airwaves either for that matter. I never listen to the radio as I can't stand modern chart music. Had I been listening, of course, I might have realised what was going on around me. But I wasn't, so I didn't.

Life's a bitch, and then you die. Or is it life's a bitch, then you marry one? Either way, looking back I guess it was only a matter of time before some conscientious member of the public decided to call the cops and let them know that public enemy number one was on the M6 heading north.

Traffic was fairly light in the early part of my journey, and that, coupled with the weather, is probably the reason it took so long for someone to spot my car and realise it was the one they were talking about on the radio. In fact, I was well over halfway to my destination before it happened.

That, along with the police trying to organise which force would be the best one to try to intercept me as they couldn't know where I was heading or when I was likely to come off the motorway, gave me an opportunity to get a lot further along. Then some off duty cop got on my tail and decided to do the decent thing and tell his colleagues that he would follow me carefully to wherever I was heading, and then call them again when I stopped.

This meant that there was no need for a potential high-speed chase, which I guess no one really fancied in the weather conditions. All they'd have to do would be to pull up by my car when I left it and wait for me to come back to it again. How hard could it be?

So I was basically allowed to continue to my destination unhindered, which, as stated, was somewhere I didn't really want to go. I had to be there though, whether I wanted to or not. It was important, vitally important even, that I get there.

I got to where I was going just before 11am, which meant I'd made it by the skin of my teeth. I never once noticed the green BMW behind me, even though it turned out he'd been tailing me for over 100 miles. I pulled up outside the gates and made my way inside, finding my seat just in time for it to all start.

I was there for nearly an hour, doing what I had to do, even though it was the hardest thing I've ever done. I somehow managed to keep my voice steady and strong, even when it was my turn to speak.

Truth is, I wasn't all that surprised when I walked back outside to see a police car parked up behind mine. Not surprised, but totally dismayed. There was still something else I needed to do, so I walked up to them and asked them for a little consideration.

There were two of them in the car, one male and one female, and when I explained what was going on I saw two totally different expressions on their faces. The guy seemed pretty calm about things, and was clearly willing to let me finish what I had to do before arresting me. His partner, however, showed nothing but disgust on her face.

Which, in the circumstances, I could totally understand.

The two of them had a little discussion with each other, and it was the male cop that won in the end, although perhaps it was more a compromise than a victory. I was to be allowed to do what I'd come all this way to do, but only on condition I agreed to be handcuffed to one of them while I did it.

I guess after driving from one end of the country to the other the female cop had a point when she said she considered me a flight risk.

Twenty minutes later I stood there in shame, handcuffed to WPC Griffin, as it turned out she was called, whilst they buried my son. He was 14 years old, and had been killed the week before whilst playing with friends.

The worst part about it, as far as I was concerned anyway, was that the police still hadn't managed to trace the driver who hit him.

Old Albert

My dad had just asked me if I remembered the old man who used to live down the road from us, and I was instantly transported back into a maelstrom of memories.

From the first time I'd spoken to him, to the hours spent reading with him late into the night. Bad memories, like me holding him upright at his wife's funeral. A funeral his family were 'too busy' to attend. Good memories, like the day I walked into town with him so he could watch his beloved football team bring home the FA Cup.

So many recollections, both good and bad, came flooding through my mind that I was almost overcome. I knew, as soon as my dad asked me, that it could only be bad news. In my heart I was already weeping for the passing of one of the best friends I ever had. I was distraught and allowed myself to think back a little, so at first I didn't hear what my dad went on to say.

I'd first spoken to Albert many years earlier, when I was just eleven years old. Our school had an annual harvest festival, where everyone brought in tins of food, packets of biscuits, whatever they could spare. This was then divided up into little hampers and taken around and distributed to the needy members of the community.

This particular year I was asked to nominate someone for some reason, and the first people that came to mind where the old couple that lived down the road. They always looked a shoddy pair in my mind, often wearing threadbare clothes which they sometimes didn't change for days.

Even to someone as young as I was then, it was obvious that they didn't have a lot of money, so I had no hesitation in suggesting they may be suitable recipients of one of the hampers. Of course, as it was my idea it was then me who had to deliver it.

The look on Beryl's face, as I later learned her name to be, when she answered the door and saw me stood there with a hamper full of food, was, without a doubt, the most joyous moment of my life. To see the happiness such a simple gesture could bring turned my life around, and I resolved in that instant to dedicate my life to helping others.

After the initial meeting I began to spend more and more time with the couple. I'd go and do shopping for them, tend the garden, help out with things like washing and so on. When their eyes began to feel the strain of old age I would go around each morning to read the newspaper to them. I could sense the pleasure they got from my company, and that was more than enough reward for me.

Eventually I found out about their family. They had two sons, one of whom had emigrated to Australia many years earlier, and one who was a top barrister working in London. Neither of the two sons paid their parents any attention whatsoever, which I found extremely sad and depressing.

When I was approaching my 18th birthday old Beryl passed away suddenly. There was no illness preceding it. She just went to bed one night and that was it, she never woke up.

Albert was devastated, as you might imagine after 53 years of marriage. I think what hurt even more though was that both sons insisted they were too busy to come to the funeral, no matter how much he begged them. And that was how I found myself celebrating my 18th birthday, the day I officially became a man, holding up a frail old gentleman in a crematorium.

I went to university soon after that, and although I tried my best to keep in touch with Albert through letters, phone calls and so on, eventually it all petered out, as such things tend to do.

Now my dad was asking if I remembered him, and I figured I should tune back into reality to find out what he'd died of.

"Anyway, as I was saying, Albert is getting married next week. Some lady he met in the old peoples home he lives in now. He wants to know if you'll be his best man"

I sat there and stared at the phone for a few minutes before a huge grin spread across my face, then promised to be on the next available flight home. I had a wedding to attend, and nothing was going to get in my way.

Rebecca

It was only after clicking 'send' that Rebecca realised what she'd done. She knew that this time there would be no getting around it. Rebecca was in trouble.

Not just any kind of trouble. This was to be trouble of the big, large, and nasty variety. The only word she could think of for the next fifteen minutes or so was 'ooops'.

Which, in actuality, is not even a real word. I mean, think about it. How can you have a word with three vowels followed by two consonants? If you could have words like that, for example, winning at Scrabble would be so much easier...

Anyway, I digress. Rebecca was in bother, dire straits, and hot water. It was too late now to un-send, although, even if it had not actually been too late she was not really aware of how to go about the task of un-sending anyway.

So she sat at the desk, shivering with trepidation, and awaiting the eruption of fury that was soon to arrive in her vicinity. Not usually one to worry she was, all the same, fraught with vexation.

Now, there is one thing I can say with absolute confidence. When you're waiting for something good to happen the time will drag on and on for what appears to be eternity, when in reality it's only five minutes.

Completely the opposite is true when you're expecting something bad to happen. Time seems to speed up in such cases, and, depending on the severity of the badness you're expecting time will, invariably, become faster and faster in conjunction.

This is a statement of truth, and is not disputed by even the most knowledgeable of knowledgeable people. The question that springs to mind with this factoid though is - how does time know? How does time know whether the event any particular individual is waiting for is going to be a happy or a sad event for that person? This is something that's puzzled me for many years, and probably not only me.

Yet for some reason, those knowledgeable people I mentioned earlier are not seemingly capable of explaining the finer workings of the system that we know as time.

Once more, I digress. I seem to be highly talented at digression, and not so talented at getting to the point. The point being that after what seemed like only a couple of moments to Rebecca but was, in reality, seventeen days, four hours, twenty eight minutes, and forty one seconds, the dreaded reaction she was expecting finally arrived.

She sat and stared at her computer screen, willing her e-mail inbox to be devoid of e-mail. It wasn't. She stared some more, and then considered just deleting the offending cyber document without even reading it. She couldn't.

She thought long and hard about the events set in motion by something as simple as sending an e-mail that she hadn't actually meant to send, and then realised that she wasn't, as yet, properly aware of the exactness of said events as she hadn't read the bothersome e-mail. So she resolved to do just that.

Tomorrow. Tomorrow morning. She'd read it by accident when she came into work hung over and not realise what she'd done until it was too late. Yes, tomorrow would be a fine time to read about the doom and folly set in motion by her actions. Then she thought for a few moments more before deciding that in actuality there was no time like the present and moving her curser over the e-mail folder icon.

A week later she finally got around to reading the e-mail and was shocked at what she saw. Did I say shocked? My apologies. I meant agog, startled, perplexed and mystified. Or something like that.

The e-mail that she'd been so reluctant to open, that left her aghast and agape at its contents, read as follows...

'Dear Rebecca

Many thanks for getting in contact with me. Like you, I have never before tried Internet dating, and am as worried and confused as you appear to be. However, having viewed your profile, I'd like to know more about you.

If you'd like to contact me directly, my e-mail address is (censored to protect the innocent)

I look forwards to hearing from you soon.

Timothy.

Too Young

Too young
oh much too young
Seventeen years old
no chance to live your life
to travel

your youthfullness taken
in just a moment
going from innocent
to pregnant

and now
no more friends
no more for you
Friday nights partying

just nappies
and screaming, shouting

when does it stop?
how long will it last?
maybe, if you're lucky
another 16 years, then it will be over
for a little while, until

before you're even thirty-five
you hear the word you've always dreaded

Granny

Sexist Theory

I was recently asked by a friend how it is that men can even function on a daily basis when all we ever seem to think about is sex, so I used the 11.3 spare nanoseconds I had for the day and thought seriously about how it is that guys do actually manage to get through life, despite literally thinking of nothing but sex. And football of course. After all, what man doesn't think about football 30 or 40 times a day?

I'd like to point out at this point that as I am willing to accept certain stereotypical opinions, (like all men ever think about is sex), I think it's only fair that you women out there accept some of the stereotypical opinions I'm about to mention. After all, it's only fair really!

Anyway, let's get on with things...

I think the main reason us guys function as well as we do, even though we never think of anything but sex and football, is the fact that both sex and football are things that can get your adrenalin pumping just by thinking about them, and as a result of the extra adrenalin in the blood stream we have a higher sense of what's going on around us at all times.

Which is why men are capable of things like parking correctly and women are not. We're more aware of our surroundings than women are.

The average female mind is too busy being cluttered up with things like shopping lists, laundry, ironing, feeding the kids, and trying to remember if they locked the door behind them when they left home. Trying to concentrate on too many things at once basically, and as a result struggling to actually think anything through properly to its most likely conclusion, and also unable to concentrate enough on the thing that is most important at that particular moment.

Like that gate post in the driveway that you just bumped into as you were reversing the car out onto the street.

So, my findings in this extremely exhaustive and scientific study are simple.

If women spent more time thinking about things like sex, football, and fast cars, they'd be more likely to be able to focus on what is important at any given time instead of having their minds cluttered up with trivial stuff.

Spending less time watching soap operas would probably also help, as these serve to do nothing more than rot any brain-cells that may still be active, and have even been known to cause serious diseases in women such as lackofknowledgeofrealityissues and livinginadreamlandism.

Okay, so this isn't very long. But you have to remember that I only had 11.3 nanoseconds to not only think all this, but also to type it all as well. Now I have to go off and think about sex some more. And football of course!

Coffee Stains

"Sorry about the coffee stains..."

I looked at him for a few more seconds, made a mental note of the smug grin playing over his face.

And then I shot him.

A little harsh I know, shooting someone over coffee stains, especially when he'd already apologised for them. It was more than just the coffee stains though. It was more a combination of everything together being too much for me.

Allow me to explain.

I'd been with Michelle for nearly three years when I sensed things were starting to go wrong. I don't know what it was in particular that made me suspicious. It just didn't seem the same any more.

She started to spend more time out with her friends, for one thing. Don't get me wrong, right from the very beginning she'd made it clear she valued her independence, and I wasn't going to stand in the way of that, so every Friday night she went out with her friends while I stayed at home, and on Saturdays it was my turn to go out. We'd also go out together probably two or three times during the week as neither of us particularly liked cooking.

So for three years everything was fine. Then she started to make excuses for why she couldn't spend time with me. It was no longer just Friday nights out with the girls, now she was going to the gym a couple of times a week as well.

I let it slide to begin with, which is perhaps where I went wrong. If I'd said something right at the start maybe things wouldn't have degenerated to the level they did. It's easy to have twenty-twenty vision in hindsight though.

So I let it go, figuring I wasn't going to get in her way if she wanted to spend more time with her friends. After all, it gave me more time to indulge in my hobbies, and it wasn't like we were never seeing each other any longer.

Not at first anyway.

This went on for a year or so, and gradually we saw less and less of each other. It got to the point where the only times we ever spoke was when we happened to bump into one another on the way in or out of the house.

Then it happened, the day my life fell apart.

I came home from work early, wanting to pick something up that I needed for a lecture that afternoon. When I got home I found the front door was unlocked, and there was a strange car in the drive.

I tried to call Michelle on her cell-phone but there was no response. I wanted to ask her if she was home, thinking that maybe she'd come back early for something herself and just forgotten to lock the door - the strange car could have belonged to a work colleague who'd given her a lift or something.

At least, that was how I was reasoning things at that point.

Like I said though, there was no response to my call, so I decided to go in and investigate. So I did what any law abiding citizen would do first and went to my car to retrieve my gun. Just in case.

I walked slowly around the house, not wanting to shout in case the place was being robbed and I disturbed someone. The last thing I wanted was to alert a burglar to my presence in the building.

To be honest, I think that deep down I probably suspected what I was going to find and was just trying to blank it out of my mind. I would have much preferred to run into a burglar that day, or a crowd of them, than what I eventually found in the living room.

Come to that, things would have been better if I'd just gone outside and called the cops and reported a suspected robbery in progress. Anything at all other than the actions I took, for which I can hold only myself responsible.

Anyway, having searched most of the downstairs area I headed into the living room. It was here that the nightmare that had been hiding itself at the back of my mind for the last six or seven months finally manifested itself in reality, along with the reason Michelle, the only woman I ever truly loved, had been spending so much time at the gym.

The two of them were on the couch together, Michelle and an absolute giant of a man. One look at him was enough for me to deduce that he'd almost certainly been popping steroids from an early age, because it's just not possible to get a physique like that naturally.

He was lying with Michelle, both of them naked, and both of them clearly reaching the end of a very heavy session of love making judging by the amount they were both sweating. All I could see were the two bodies moving seemingly in slow motion, all I could hear were grunts of pleasure somewhere in the background, and my mind went blank.

I have no idea how long I stood and watched them both. It could have been an hour, or just a few seconds. Time stood still for me then. I had no concept of reality at all. I was, to all intents and purposes, nothing more than an empty shell, human shaped, standing there in the room trying to take things in.

I started to look around the room, trying to find something to focus on, something that could rouse me from the trance I was in. It was all to no avail though, at least until I saw the cups.

Two coffee cups, side by side on the floor near the end of the sofa. They'd both been kicked over at some point in time, probably by the two of them as they decided they couldn't keep their hands off one another any longer, which was bad enough.

What really made me focus though, the thing that finally dragged me out of my trance and back into something resembling the real world, was when I saw where the spilt coffee had ended up. It had slowly seeped its way across the carpet until it reached the base of the chair opposite the sofa.

Or perhaps I should say, the base of the chair opposite the sofa where I had left my most prized possession that morning. And the coffee had worked its way into said prized possession, which was, in actual fact, a baseball glove.

Okay, it's only a baseball glove. So what's the fuss, I hear you ask. Well, this wasn't just any old baseball glove. This glove was the one worn by Babe Ruth in his final ever appearance, way back when. I wasn't much of a baseball fan to be honest, but I knew a future treasure when I saw one and had snapped this one up as soon as it came up for auction.

And now it was covered in coffee. This, more than anything else, was what brought me to my senses that day. At least, at the time I felt I'd been brought to my senses. I started to scream at the two of them.

I can't remember exact words as I wasn't really in control of myself properly at the time. I know I called Michelle a slut, and couldn't help but call the muscle man a junked up, pumped up freak, but apart from that I have no real recollection.

Except for my final sentence, that is. Which actually seemed to last a lot longer than any normal sentence, as I managed to ask Michelle what I'd done to deserve this treatment, ask why she felt the need to do it at home, point out the damage to my prized baseball glove, and even ask if either of them had anything to say in their defence.

At which point, muscle head looked at me, looked at the glove, looked at me again, smiled, and said...

"Sorry about the coffee stains..."

I Hate Umbrellas

I hate umbrellas. There is, on the surface of it, no rational explanation for this aversion to what, at first glance, is nothing more than a handy implement for keeping your hair dry in the rain, yet I abhor them all the same. I'll try to explain why.

First off, I should point out that at six foot one high I'm taller than your average umbrella user. I also, as a result of my height, have quite long legs. Now, I think it's something to do with physics, although I may be mistaken, but my long legs actually result in a rather fast walking pace.

Now, if you can I'd like you to picture a certain scenario. What we have in front of us is a street. Not a particularly impressive street, but one thing that we should notice is that it's pedestrianized – which means there are no cars allowed on it for the Americans reading this.

On either side of this pedestrianised street there are shops along the whole length, and the length of the street is about half a mile. The shops are nothing special, by the way, just your normal, run of the mill, high street stores.

Now, imagine it's a Saturday, probably somewhere around 3pm, and as is traditional for pedestrianised streets full of normal, run of the mill, high street stores at 3pm on a Saturday, this one is full of people. Lots of people actually, who as luck would have it seem to be of all different sizes.

Many of these people will be children. The majority of them will almost certainly be female. And each and every one of them is doing the same thing - shopping. Because it's Saturday, and everybody goes shopping on Saturday.

Okay, so far, so good - I'm hoping you're all still with me, so now it's time for a little more detail. Anyone that has long legs, or walks at anything above an average pace, will tell you that streets such as this can be extremely hazardous.

At first glance there's nothing to fear from such a location, until you apply basic physics that is. (At least, I think it's physics. Science was never my strong subject at school. Come to think of it, school was never my strong subject at school).

Anyway, I digress. The reason such a street can be so treacherous is as follows. First off, assume the following three statements to be true.

Every single person walks at their own individual pace.

People with long legs walk faster than people with short legs.

As a result, the people with the long legs will always overtake people with short legs travelling in the same direction.

No problems following my logic so far I expect. Now pay attention, because this is where it starts to get complicated.

Have you ever noticed how people who are out shopping will, quite regularly and suddenly, stop walking? I don't mean slow down, or glance around and wait for a friend to catch up, by the way, I mean quite simply, stop. Totally stop - in the middle of the street. Maybe they just saw something out of the corner of their eye in a shop and need to go for another look or something. Whatever - they stop, suddenly and without warning I can assure you. Especially women.

So now, imagine you have long legs and are walking close behind someone in a crowded street and they stop suddenly. What do you do?

Well, speaking personally I long ago perfected the hip-swing, which, as soon as someone either stops dead or suddenly changes direction in front of me means I swing my hips and breeze right past them. I'm actually so good at this move that I can almost do it without thinking about it. Most of the time anyway.

The problem begins when it starts to rain.

When it rains the umbrellas appear. I have no idea where they appear from so suddenly, but they do. I don't even know why, as I don't recall ever hearing of anyone dropping down dead of pneumonia because they got their hair wet going to Tesco's for a pint of milk.

Still, the damn things appear. And they're dangerous. You don't believe me? Think about it.

Have you ever noticed how the canvas bit, the part that opens out and goes over your head to keep you dry, is held in shape? No? Well, I'll tell you then - metal rods running from the top of the handle to the end of the canvas. Or, in fact, to just beyond the end of the canvas, so there's a little bit of each metal rod poking out.

Still, that's not exactly dangerous, right? Wrong. You see, the problem is, for someone like me anyway who is slightly taller than average and certainly taller than most women, is that most of these little bits of metal rod that are poking out are at the same level, which is eye level. For me anyway.

Okay, so, no big problem, all I have to do is not be stupid enough to walk into the back of an umbrella and my eyesight is perfectly safe. This is easier said than done though, especially when you take into account all those people who just stop dead in the middle of the street.

And the hip-swerve doesn't work with umbrellas because they stretch out over the top of a persons shoulders and then go a little bit further still, so I have to swerve further out to get past them or I get a piece of metal in my eye.

But then it gets worse, because as soon I swerve to avoid the silly cow who just spotted a lovely pair of shoes that she can't afford anyway, there's another one coming up in the opposite direction. And she's probably going to turn to the side to speak to someone or look at something as soon as I start to go past her.

If you ever stand somewhere that allows you a chance to look down on a street of shops from above when it's raining, I can assure you that you'll have a birds eye view of lots of men walking down the street ducking and diving and dodging from side to side. Constantly weaving, left, right, left, left right.

Mohammed Ali never learned to fight like he did in a boxing ring. He did it on Saturday afternoons avoiding stupid women and their umbrellas.

And if he didn't, he should have!

Vengeance

He came out of the store and turned to his left, which was a good start as it meant he was walking away from me, and so gave me at least a chance to launch a surprise attack.

I stood up in the doorway I'd been crouching in for the last twenty minutes or so, waiting for him to finish. I looked around, made sure no-one was paying me any undue attention, and started to follow him.

He was a few hundred feet in front of me by now, but I knew it would only take me a little while to catch up. If I timed it right there was an alleyway that he tended to cut through on his way home, and at this time of night it should be deserted. All I had to do was be close enough to attack when the time came.

I pulled my hood down over my face, just in case he looked back and recognised me. Placing my hand in my pocket I checked to make sure my weapon was still there and started to pull it out slowly. There were only a hundred yards left until he got to the alleyway now and I was still a fair way behind him, so it was time to speed up a little.

I kept my hand in my pocket as I closed the distance. I already knew that when the time came I would be able to pull out the weapon and hit him in a smooth motion - the trick was to make sure not to pull it out too soon. I didn't want to arouse the suspicion of anyone that might be watching me.

He was approaching the entry to the alleyway now, and he walked in with me just a dozen or so paces behind him. He was oblivious to my presence, or if he did realise that there was someone behind him he didn't see them as a threat. But then, he wouldn't. An action man super hero tough guy like him isn't going to feel threatened by anybody.

I got to six paces behind, five, four. I pulled my hand out of my pocket, revealing my weapon of choice. It was a bottle - a very heavy and very solid bottle. I was assuming it would shatter when I hit him with it, although to be honest I wasn't going to be that bothered if it didn't.

I got to a couple of paces behind him and he started to finally realise something may be wrong. It was too late though. As he began to turn around I raised the bottle over my head and brought it down on top of his with as much force as I could manage.

I was expecting the bottle to smash, to hear a loud noise and see plenty of blood. All I heard though was a dull thud, and then he dropped to the ground in front of me. I bent over him and felt for a pulse, but couldn't find one. Damn. I think I might have gone too far with this one. I tried to think for a minute or so about the best way to handle the situation.

I reached over him to turn him onto his back, then put my hand into the right front pocket of his jeans and removed his wallet. That was good, now it was going to look like a mugging gone wrong. The next priority was the clean getaway. I walked on towards the opposite end of the alley to where I came in, as turning around could look suspicious if there was anyone watching the entrance for any reason.

After about fifteen steps or so I stopped and turned back, then went back to him, lying there in the alleyway. There was no sign of any marks or bruising as yet, which I didn't think was a good sign for me. I picked up the bottle from where it had fallen at the side of him. Even the collision with the concrete pavement didn't break the damn thing.

I took a quick look around to make sure there was no-one watching me, then headed to the end of the alleyway, having first hidden the bottle in my pocket again. About half a mile down the road I dropped the bottle into a dustbin, having first smashed it against the inside of the metal bin so it wouldn't arouse suspicion if it was found intact.

I then took the money out of his wallet and placed it into mine. I got on four different buses in the next half an hour and eventually found one that was quiet enough for me to drop his wallet to the floor without anyone noticing. I knew it was going to be found, but it was just going to send the police off in the wrong direction. The bus I dropped it on didn't go within even twenty miles of where I lived. A few stops later I got off and made my way back into town.

By the time I got home it was on the news already. A body had been found in an alleyway, appeared to be a mugging gone wrong, there were no clues as yet and the police were appealing for witnesses. As I sat down and watched the news I thought back on the events that led to me killing someone...
- -

Anthony Jackson joined the company I worked for on the 21st June 2005. From the moment I met him there was something about him that I didn't like. I couldn't put my finger on what it was, as he was always pleasant to everyone, and was certainly good at his job. There was just an air of smugness about him, something that implied that he was laughing at us all behind our backs.

I know I wasn't the only person who felt this way about him, although I was certainly less trusting of him than anyone else. I was also the only person that never quite got over that initial feeling of mistrust.

Things were probably not helped when I found out that he was dating Martina. I can already hear you wanting to ask who Martina was, so here goes. She worked in Customer Services in our company, and the truth was that from the moment I met her I had a huge crush on her.

Don't get me wrong, she wasn't a classic beauty or anything like that. She was 5ft 3 tall and had short brown hair, brown eyes, and could probably do with losing a few pounds. Not a lot, mind, but she was clearly not in perfect shape. The fact that she wore glasses would put most guys off her as well, but I'm not like that.

Anyway, by the time her boyfriend Anthony joined the company, Martina and I were firm friends. We'd even been out a few times after work for a drink, but it was strictly platonic between us. I'd have preferred it not to be, but I didn't see the point in rushing things. If she was interested in me in that way I figured she'd let me know sooner or later, and there was no point spoiling the friendship for something that might not happen.

And then her boyfriend turned up. I'd like to point out at this point that I couldn't stand him way before I found out he was going out with her. Okay, that maybe didn't help me get over my original feelings, but the original feelings were not even remotely jealousy related.

Things kind of carried on for a year or so with not much changing. Martina and I were still great friends, and I never bothered telling her my feelings about Anthony as I figured she'd just see it as me trying to make trouble for her.

Even when I found out he was screwing around behind her back I didn't say anything to her as I was afraid she'd see right through to my main reason for wanting her to dump him and call me a liar or something. No, I figured I'd just make sure I stayed friends with her so I could be there to pick up the pieces when she eventually found out.

Which of course she did, and then she fell apart, just totally disintegrated. And like the friend I was I made sure I stayed around to help her out.

Now, I know what you're thinking, because if I was reading this I'd be thinking the same. You're thinking that I pretended to be her friend all that time so that I could take advantage of her when she was feeling low and depressed. And I don't blame you for thinking that either. I'd like to put it on record though that I'm not that kind of guy.

About a week after she broke up with Anthony, she came out with me for a drink after work. We sat in the back room of the pub and just talked for a couple of hours before I walked her to the bus stop, which was our normal routine. Once there she got all upset about going home alone and I gave her a hug, and the next thing I knew she was kissing me.

In other circumstances this would have been my dream come true. Right then though, it was wrong. I knew it was wrong, and I told her it was wrong, and then of course I had to go through the whole scene of 'I thought you liked me' and stuff.

At which point, like the true gentleman I am of course, I told her exactly how I felt about her. Then I explained that although I'd like nothing more than to be the guy she woke up to every morning, right now it was the wrong time, place, and circumstances to set something like that in motion. She needed to get over Anthony first, and then if she still wanted me to be something other than just a friend, I'd be happy to oblige.

We separated that night with a hug and a peck on the cheek, and she thanked me for being so understanding and careful with her. We remained friends, but never really managed to get beyond that. I know I made the right decision that night though.

Anyway, on with the tale. A week or so later when we all got paid practically the whole company did what we always did on a Friday night and went to the pub to get wasted.

By now, it was no surprise to anyone to see Martina and I go and sit in a corner and just chat amongst ourselves. Friends did that kind of thing all the time, and it didn't take a rocket scientist to see that all we were was friends. Unfortunately, that night it wasn't a rocket scientist watching us.

It was Anthony. For about three hours he stood and stared and watched the two of us laughing and joking together. If I'd known this at the time I would have done things differently that night. But these things are always easier with hindsight.

At about ten o clock, I walked Martina to the bus stop. As I already said, this was a weekly ritual we had, like friends do, and i made sure she got on the bus okay then walked around the corner to my mothers pub for a few more pints.

I hadn't been in the pub for five minutes when the door opened and Anthony walked in. He didn't look happy about something, and to this day I wish I'd read the signs differently and not answered him truthfully when he asked where Martina was.

"She's on the bus on the way home. Why?"

He didn't answer, just stormed back out of the door and jumped into a taxi that was waiting for him outside.

It took me a few seconds to put two and two together, but as soon as I did I wasn't impressed with the answer I came up with. I sprinted out of the pub myself and ran to try and get a taxi.

About twenty minutes later I pulled up outside Martina's house in the taxi. I had a look around but there were no lights on. I knocked on the door but there was no answer. I put my ear to the door to see if I could hear anything inside, but again there was nothing.

I went around to the back of the house and followed the same routine, with the same results. The house was in darkness, the doors were secure, no one was answering my knocks, and no sounds were coming from inside.

I'd like to think the conclusion I came to was the one everybody else would come to in those circumstances. Martina was asleep in bed, and Anthony, once he'd found out she wasn't with me, had gone home. It seemed a perfectly reasonable solution to me, so I headed home myself.

It was three weeks before I saw Martina again, three weeks where nobody knew where she was or what had happened to her. By the time she did come back to work most of the bruising had gone. The external bruising anyway, and it was another month before she told me what had happened that night.

A few minutes after she got home she'd heard a knock on the door. Going to answer it she'd paused for a second to ask who it was. It was Anthony, and he wanted to talk, and at this time she still had pretty strong feelings for him so she let him in.

As soon as he was through the door though he punched her in the face, and then closing the door behind him he proceeded to kick and punch her until she was unconscious. When she came around she was upstairs in her bedroom, and he'd gagged her, and was raping her. In the background she could hear me knocking on the door, but the gag meant she couldn't cry out.

He spent most of the night doing unspeakable things to her. At about 5am he untied her and walked out of the room. It was three days before she could even bring herself to get out of bed, and another week before she could walk properly.

Anthony Jackson was arrested, interviewed, and then released without charge. One of the other girls from work gave him an alibi, claiming he'd been with her all night.

Six weeks later he did the same thing to her, and she refused to press charges because she felt like an idiot for backing him up the first time. And she still loved him of course. Go figure.
- -

So I sat there watching the news and thought about Anthony Jackson. I hadn't meant to kill him, but the more I thought about it the more I was glad he was dead. At least now he'd never be able to hurt another woman.

As for Martina, by this time, she'd been married for three years. There were no kids as yet, but she was hoping to be accepted for fertility treatment. She'd been sterile ever since that night of terror, but at least she'd finally found a guy that she loved, and who loved her.

Unfortunately it wasn't me, but at least I'd gotten some form of revenge for her, even if I couldn't tell her about it. Just in case.

The Tunnel of Death

They came at dawn to take me
From solitary, where I'd been held
Four armed guards, unsmiling
In my hands my head was held

They walked me through the courtyard
Beneath the blazing sun,
While all around were prisoners
Working at the point of a gun

They led me to the tunnel
From which no-one returned
Descending into darkness
Behind me bridges burned

My crime was but a small one
For my child I stole some bread
My payment would be massive
Within moments I'd be dead

We marched in single file
With just a torch to guide
Several times I blundered
As I paced along near blind

The tunnel twisted and turned
I knew not where it led
At least the walls weren't so low
As to make me bang my head

Ahead I saw some daylight
And I knew the end was near
Emerging into sunlight
I tried hard to fight back tears

We marched towards the gallows
Where some poor man was hung
I took my place beside himas
A bell of death was rung

There were no words or speeches
In silence I was strung
High upon the scaffold
At twenty-two years young

Janie's Got a Gun

I was ten years old the first time it happened. I was sleeping in my new bedroom, the one I finally had all to myself now that our family had just moved into a new house. It was because of my mothers new husband that we'd moved of course, and he seemed a nice enough guy.

Right up until the night I woke up to find him touching me.

I thought I was imagining it at first. I mean, there I was, ten years old, old terrycloth nightgown on, and my step-dad was touching me. And I don't mean touching me in an innocent way, like parents do to kids all the time. I mean he was rubbing me between my legs, which was totally weird because I just didn't understand why he would be doing something like that.

I mean, I hadn't started to develop yet so it certainly wasn't doing anything for me apart from being an unpleasant feeling, and I didn't know anything about sex yet either so I couldn't think what it could be doing for him.

I did notice his face was flushed, and that he seemed very excited about something, but what it was that caused his excitement was beyond me. At least then it was beyond me anyway. Later on, of course, I would learn all about his sick perversions, but right then I was still innocent.

That first night he came into my room all he did was rub me between my legs for a few minutes. I don't think he even realised I was awake, as I was too scared to move when I woke up. I didn't say anything either, to him then, or to anyone else the next day. I thought maybe it had all been some sort of dream or something.

So I kept it to myself. And then a few nights later when I woke up to him kissing me, breath stinking of beer, I never said anything about that either. I guess I was in some sort of denial or something, thinking that it couldn't really be happening to me.

I mean, the man who had just married my mother was in my bedroom at night, kissing me. It just didn't make any sense to me. Even now I can't understand it, so what chance did I have then?

When I was thirteen years old I told my mother that her husband was coming into my room at night. She told me it was nothing abnormal and that he was just coming in to make sure I was okay. When I told her some of the things he was actually doing to me when he came in to 'check I was okay', she went mad and told me to stop telling filthy lies, asking me which of my friends had put me up to it. It was quite clear at that moment that she was never going to believe anything negative I said about her beloved husband.

And truth be told, why should she believe me? I could hardly believe it myself, and it had been going on for over three years already, and for the last two he'd been having me touch him back, making me hold him and caress him and stuff.

I felt dirty, depressed, and used. I wanted to know what I'd done to deserve this treatment from him. I mean, clearly I must have done something, I just couldn't work out what it was. I was approaching breaking point, and deep down I knew that something had to change before it was too late.

It was one of my school friends who offered the solution, albeit unwittingly. I was approaching my sixteenth birthday, and staying over with her for a few days while my parents were away. She lived in a big house and we pretty much had the run of the whole place, apart from one room.

There was just one room in the house I wasn't allowed in under any circumstances, so being a normal, healthy, curious teenager I asked what was in there that was so important.

This is when she told me that it was her fathers gun room, and it was also around about this time that I started to see a possible end to the abuse I was suffering at home. Of course, I didn't tell my friend what was going on in my mind. She wouldn't have understood anyway, as she didn't know about what went on when I was in bed at night.

After the reaction I got from my mother when I told her, I hadn't seen any point in confiding in anyone else, as I was sure they'd only react in the same way and accuse me of making it all up or something. So I kept quiet. Maybe if I'd had the guts to speak to someone about it things would have turned out differently. Who can tell?

On the night of my sixteenth birthday he came to my room for the last time. He'd been telling me for months that he had something special planned for my birthday, and the way he looked at my ass when I walked past him gave me some idea of what his 'something special' was all about.

What he didn't know, of course, was that I had something special planned for him as well. I'd stolen one of the guns from my friends house that afternoon. I'd also managed to find a couple of bullets in one of the drawers, and had fired a practice shot on the way home in the woods to make sure it worked.

So he came into my room as I said, and then stood at the foot of my bed and got undressed as he always had done before. The site of his naked body had always repulsed me, but this time I smiled at him, and he smiled back as he climbed into the bed beside me.

His smile that was still changing to a look of shock when the bullet entered the front of his head, and it still hadn't made it all the way there when the bullet exited from the back of his head and buried itself in the bedroom wall.

The room was a mess, with blood and brain matter everywhere. I could feel something warm and wet on my face, which any other time would surely have made me physically sick, but I was lying there grinning when my mother entered the room to see what was going on.

It was over. I was free from his evil.

Don't Cry

Letting go is the hardest part I think, finally accepting that it's actually over and that they aren't coming back. It was always going to be hard anyway, circumstances being as they were, but it was made even harder by the fact that she never even left a note telling me what her reasons were.

So I guess you could say I was a prime candidate for the funny farm when I didn't get a note. Although, truth be told, I was probably a prime candidate for the funny farm from the day I got beat up by my mother for doing as I was told.

I mean, getting beat up when I did something wrong, or when I deliberately ignored an instruction or something, that was fine. Obviously I didn't like it much, but I knew I deserved it so I just took my punishment and got on with things.

Like the time my mum heard me swearing and decided to wash my mouth out with a bar of soap. Okay, in hindsight, she was probably a little more forceful than she meant to be, but those two teeth were on the verge of falling out anyway. And it was still my first set of teeth, so it didn't really matter because they soon grew back.

So like I said, when I did something wrong I accepted the punishment issued and got on with things. But when you do as your mother tells you and still get punished, I don't think anyone can argue that I was bound to grow up confused.

Again, playing on the motorway, in hindsight, was probably not the greatest plan a five year old kid ever came up with.

But she told me to do it, and I did as I was told. Ergo, she had no damn right to beat the hell out of me over it! Still, like I said, I guess I was a contender for the nut house from that day onwards.

That didn't mean I was going to go easily. With or without that stupid note I was never going to lie down and just take it. Not a chance. Not me. I'm better than that. Always was, always will be, or so I thought at the time. Clearly, over time it did all get to me, probably a little more than it should have done.

That's not bad, not even at the end of the first page yet and already up to my third case of hindsight. Which, believe it or not, is not now and never has been my word of the day, it just seems to keep cropping up all of a sudden for some reason. Maybe when I look back on things it'll make more sense.

Anyway, the note, or the lack of one. The note that would have explained her actions and how it was all my fault. I was too self centred probably, too busy doing my own things to notice what she was going through, and more interested in going out with the lads on a Friday night than in paying her the attention she deserved.

When we first met we used to go out for long walks in the park together, just the two of us. One of the first things I noticed about her was what a great listener she was. I could go on for hours about problems I was having at work and she'd just walk along beside me listening to everything I had to say. No matter how much I talked about my problems, she never complained once about it.

Of course, over time the walks became less frequent, but that's just natural, right? I mean, as the relationship developed we became more comfortable with each others company and stuff, and most of the things we needed to say to each other were said in those first few months.

She used to be waiting for me when I came home from work every night. Always there for me, no matter how late I was. If she smelled any of the others I got involved with occasionally, or had any inkling that I was spending quality time with other females, she never let on about it, she was just always there for me when I came home, and she didn't seem to mind if I wanted to go straight out after work either, as long as she could come with me.

I don't think I ever really knew how much I loved her until she was gone, and by then of course it was too late.

I know I wasn't as good to her as I could have been. Or, indeed, probably should have been. I tried my best, but I guess I always had other priorities, one of which was football. Don't get me wrong, she seemed to like football herself, and she'd happily sit down with me on a Sunday afternoon and watch the match on Sky, and she was always just as excited as me on Cup Final day when all the guys came round.

I used to think about taking her along to the match sometimes, rather than leave her at home. But I know my friends would have ripped the shit out of me if I'd have turned up outside the ground with her in tow. They couldn't understand what it was like for the two of us as it was.

I did take her to the pub at least. Admittedly, mainly only in the afternoons when I had a day off work, and as far as I can recall I never actually took her to my local. Probably scared of how my mates would react if they saw the two of us walk through the door together or something.

I was stupid really, as I should have just taken her in there with me and if the guys couldn't accept her as part of our crowd then clearly they weren't the friends I thought they were. And the probability is that they would have accepted her without problems anyway. I just never had the nerve to find out.

There's that hindsight thing again. Actually, I know my friends would have accepted her. Hell, the fact that they all do nothing but ask if I've had any news since she vanished makes it clear that they cared for her as well.

Not as much as me of course. No-one could care for her like I did. But then, they did usually only see her when there was a big football match on the TV anyway, so they knew her, but not the way I knew her. Maybe that was part of the problem. I should have involved her more when I was doing things with the guys.

She's been gone for nearly a month now. I had no indication there was anything wrong in advance. She was there at the door to see me off when I went to work in the morning, and no longer there when I got home.

I didn't panic at first of course, figuring she'd just gone out for a walk or something, but when she still wasn't back at nine o'clock that night I started to suspect there was something wrong. So I called up everyone I knew, asking if they'd seen her. No-one had.

And now, still no-one's seen her. Where did she go? Why did she go? Is she okay or has she had an accident somewhere? All questions that run through my mind probably a couple of hundred times a day, questions that I'm starting to think I'll never get satisfactory answers to.

I just hope that wherever she is, she's happy. If nothing else, she deserves to be happy.

No, I think she's moved on to a better place. She's found someone else to give her the love and attention I couldn't find the time to give myself. At least, this is what I hope. Maybe one day I'll find out for sure, but in the meantime I live in hope.

God I loved that dog!

Hallowed be Thy Name

I don't want to die. I'm not ready to die yet, but it isn't my decision. They'll be coming to get me soon, and when they do come I want to try and be brave. I want to walk down that corridor with my head held high and send a message out that I'm not afraid of what is in store for me.

I'm not sure I'll be able to do it though because I'm absolutely terrified. Not of the pain, because I know it isn't going to hurt, or at least, it won't hurt all that much anyway. It's the dying I'm afraid of. I think we all know deep down that one day our lives will be over. It's the knowing the precise time and date of your death, that's what makes this whole system so cruel.

I was always a supporter of the death penalty, and even now, when it's almost my turn I find it hard to condemn the idea. What I do condemn though is the way that it's done. I've known now for nearly two years the precise time that I'm going to die. That kind of knowledge preys on a person, weighs them down. It can, and sometimes does, send people insane.

Can you imagine waking up each morning and knowing exactly how many more mornings you're going to wake up on? It's a terrible punishment, cruel to the extreme. Like I said, I support the death penalty and always have. But I can't support it like this. It should just be a simple procedure.

Have the trial, and if you're found guilty the sentence is passed, and then you have the right to an appeal but you should only be allowed to appeal once. None of this 'keep on appealing until you've gone to the highest court in the land' rubbish. That's just delaying the inevitable. One appeal, and if that fails you should be executed at the earliest opportunity. That way it's over and done with.

The way it's done now is cruel, no two ways about it. Not just to the rapists and the killers who are lining up like cattle waiting for their turn to be pushed into the abattoir, but for the victims too. They want closure, they just want things to be over and done with. I know one guy who's been on death row for seventeen years now, and every time he loses an appeal he just digs up grounds for a new one. He's probably going to end up dying of natural causes at this rate.

In the meantime, three of the women he raped have committed suicide because they could no longer live with what happened to them. If they'd had closure, if they could have seen him swing from that rope, perhaps they'd still be alive. Instead, every time they were expecting everything to be over and done with he launched another appeal, and their hopes were dashed once more.

I can't condone a system that allows a piece of scum like him to live on when there are innocent people out there who don't get the same benefits. The victims are the ones I feel truly sorry for, and unlike most of the people in this block I regret what I did. I don't regret it because I'm going to die for it. I regret it because it was wrong.

Of course, it's too late now to do anything about it, to change the course of events and undo what I did. It's over, it's done, and nothing I do or say now will change that. I've had a lot of time to think things through while I've been in here, and there could only ever be one conclusion to my thoughts.

What I did was wrong, seriously and totally wrong. The pain I put those two girls through, their misery and suffering, is something that I regret so much that it hurts me now to even think about it. I could try to make up excuses, claim temporary insanity or something, but I don't see that there's any point.

I'm the bad guy here. I know it and I accept it. I don't want sympathy from anyone, although if you wish to feel sorry for someone then let it be those two girls families, or the three women I mentioned earlier that couldn't live with what happened to them. Feel for the victims, because they're the ones that truly suffer through all of this.

Yes, it's been hard for me to wake up each morning knowing when I'm going to die, and I know of at least two guys while I've been here who have been gibbering, insane wrecks by the time they were taken and put out of their misery. But harder than waking up each day with the knowledge of when I'm going to die has been waking up each day with the knowledge of what I did.

It's a truly rare thing for someone in my position to accept responsibility for what they did, as the basic human survival instinct tends to take over and you try to claim it wasn't you, you were framed, anything you can think of to delay the inevitable. Nobody wants to die, yet everybody has to die at some point.

What matters now is how we choose to meet our death. Do we walk proudly up to it and shake its hand as we smile and welcome it, or do we try to run away and hide, try to escape it. I've had a couple of years to think about this and I've decided that the only proper option is to embrace and accept my impending doom. I deserve to die, my victims deserve closure.

The guards are here now and I'm starting my final walk. I stand up tall, looking as proud as I can. Not proud of what I have done, never that, but instead proud of the fact I can accept what I did and know that I was wrong. Proud to go and meet my maker and face whatever judgment there is waiting for me on the other side.

It's time now, and they're strapping me to the bed, preparing me for the injection. The doctor rubs my arm, brings up a vein, and then starts to prepare the needle. Why is it that they always use a brand new needle for everyone, by the way? It's not like we have to be worried about catching AIDS or anything! This is going to be one of my last ever thoughts.

The injection is delivered and I feel myself starting to become drowsy. A tear escapes and starts to run down my face as I look towards the mirror opposite, which I know is two-way glass and has the families of my victims behind it. Summoning up the last of my strength I lift my head and speak the last two words of my life.

"I'm sorry"

Then it's over, and I'm gone.

Axe Murder

"You're not an axe murderer, are you?"

This is a question that any guy who has ever been innocently, or even not so innocently, chatting to a female member of the species on-line will almost certainly have heard at least once in his life. Being a person who spends a lot of time innocently chatting to members of the fairer sex on-line I have been asked this question many times, and as a result I started to think about why this question gets asked so often.

And what, exactly, constitutes an axe murderer?

I think this is the crux of the matter, thus making it the main subject for debate at the moment. Many men have been accused of the crime, and almost all of them have been innocent. In fact, I'm even inclined to say that none of the men, or indeed occasional women, who have ever been accused of being an axe murderer were actually guilty of the crime of which they were accused.

I, for one, am certainly innocent of such an accusation, and no matter how many times people want to ask me, or how low my life may become at some point in the future due to as yet impossible to foresee circumstances, I can see no likelihood or situation whereby I might ever become someone that is an axe murderer.

You see, I've found a flaw in the whole 'axe murderer' thing, something that convinces me that the phenomena known as axe murderers is really just a fallacy designed to make young girls worry about the kind of guys they're associated with, and have actually deduced that there has never, in fact, been any properly recorded or documented case of axe murdering by any man, or woman, or even child.

There is a basic fact that most people seem to ignore when they talk about this subject, and I think it's an important piece of information, which, by virtue of being discarded so blithely, has led to the subject getting much more press than it should ever actually have warranted.

I feel it is my duty, now that this information has come to my attention, to point this out in order that people can stop asking such a question, and, by so doing, automatically sullying the reputation of the poor person being constantly on the receiving end of such a factually inept query.

So, I hear you ask. What is this spellbinding piece of new information that has seemingly been swept under the carpet for all these years? What could you possibly have discovered that makes you so convinced that there has never, throughout history, been a single, properly documented, axe murder?

Well, here goes, and prepare yourself, as you are going to be shocked, nay, amazed at the simplicity of the whole thing.

There is no such thing as an axe murderer, quite simply because, whilst being a very useful tool in many ways, an axe is actually an inanimate object and is therefore clearly not alive, and as such your basic axe is actually impossible to murder!

A Week of Tearing Up

I'm feeling sad, so remarkably, unbelievably sad.

I've been with this family for over 8 years now, ever since I was removed from my second family after being used as an ashtray by people. This followed my first family, where I was beaten and locked in a dark room for what seemed like days at a time for the smallest transgression.

But now I have to leave them in a few days and I really don't want to go. Life sucks, this sucks. I'm so unhappy right now that it's all I can do not to cry.

We went to the park today. I've always loved the park - When I was first brought here I was too young to really appreciate it, but I know I always got excited when I heard the word 'park'. I used to love playing with the ducks in the pond when I was little, but a few years ago the council decided to fill the pond with concrete and build flats where it used to be, all in the name of progress apparently.

Well, in my opinion progress sucks.

I really don't want to leave my family behind. I think I may be officially depressed.

When I first came here I found it so hard to trust these people. I was certain that the abuse I had grown so used to would start again at any moment, and that no matter what I did I knew it would be wrong and I'd be punished, but over time I came to realise that not every family has the same dynamic as the first two I was with. Some families actually use love and affection as their main basis of communication as opposed to hatred and bullying.

It took me over a year to work this out, and during that time I lashed out at my family so many times I lost count, even though they never did anything wrong. At the time I felt I was defending myself, and maybe I was. My main thought process at the time was "don't get too close and attached", because I knew that sooner or later these people would stop being nice to me and would start lashing out and blaming me for everything anyway, so surely it was better to just get the transition period out of the way.

But they always treated me with such a calm attitude, even when I was really badly behaved. I grew to learn that there are ways to punish bad behaviour without violence, and that these are much more effective. Before I even realised it, all I wanted more than anything else was to show my new family that I was worthy of the attention and love they were showing me.

Now I have to leave them, and that hurts. Sometimes I wonder if they can hear my stifled cries at night.

We went to the beach today, the whole family. I've always loved the beach, almost as much as the park, although not quite as much as I could have I think as we never really came here often enough for me to get to know each nook and cranny of the place like I do the park.

But still, we came enough for me to get used to playing in the surf, then lounging on the sand and relaxing at the end of a fun filled day. I'm going to miss this place the most I think, even though it isn't my favourite place. As we drove away I couldn't help looking back with a tear in my eye.

I heard my mother and father, or at least the people I now consider to be my mother and father, talking about me today. They were talking about how they're going to cope when I'm gone, and how long they think they should wait before taking someone else like me in. My mother was crying, and my dad sounded pretty hoarse too. I don't know if I'm happy or sad that it seems like they're going to miss me so much when I'm gone.

Part of me is happy, because it means that they clearly love me as much as I always thought they did, meaning that this whole thing wasn't an act all this time. But the other part of me wishes they were like my other families right now, vile people who weren't even remotely upset when I left, as I really don't want to be the source of their sadness.

Today is my last day here, and I've spent most of it in the garden, just lounging around and being generally depressed. I can see the family looking at me when they think my attention is distracted by something shiny elsewhere, and I've heard crying come from the house at least twice today. It's all I can do to keep my own wits about me right now, as I'm just as broken up about leaving as they are. Maybe more so, because at least they still get to have their nice house in a great neighbourhood once I'm gone.

Me? I have no idea what comes next.

I'm feeling tired now so I go and lie down by the pool (Yes, my family has their own pool, a scene of endless fun when I was younger), but now I'm tired so I just lie there and go to sleep.

I don't even hear it when they start calling my name. I'm dead to the world by then.

"Is he dead?"

"Yes."

"Do you think we can bury him before the kids wake up? Maybe tell them he ran away in the night?"

"I'll put him in the car and take him out of town somewhere so the kids don't see the mound in the garden and work it out. They're not idiots though and they know he was sick."

"I know, poor dog..."

Obsession

Who is she?

Every time I turn around she's there again. My friends seem
to know her, or at least, I think they do anyway. Whichever
bar we're in she just turns up and sits down with us, yet they
haven't introduced me to her, which is strange as normally
I'm introduced to anyone new that joins the group
immediately.

I'd ask myself, but it seems impolite, especially as I don't
even speak the same language as her. I resolve, once again,
that I'm going to have to learn to speak Czech when I get
back home next week.

It's just so damned hard though as there isn't anywhere I
know of back home that I can learn it. I can learn Spanish,
French, or German, sure, or Italian, Greek, or Russian, plus
about 30 different dialects of Chinese or Mandarin, but not
Czech. Although I heard Polish is a pretty similar language, so
maybe if I learn that I'd have more of a chance with basic
conversations over here. It's certainly something to look at
when I get home next week. Maybe.

Now she's on the move again. The most beautiful woman I
ever saw. (And I've seen a few, even slept with a couple). She
is undoubtedly the best though. It's hard to explain why, just
that she's perfect, and I don't even know her name, which is
so frustrating.

And then she's gone, left the building. Another opportunity
missed. Maybe later I'll have a chance to speak to her. It's

only 9.30pm, and I suspect there's at least another 7 or 8 hours drinking to look forward to yet, so I have a feeling that I haven't seen the last of her.

It's 11.30pm and we walk into a different bar, and no prizes for guessing who the first person I see when I walk through the door is. It's her again, sitting there looking as fresh as she did at lunchtime today when I first saw her, which is so damned unfair. Nobody should look that good after nearly 12 hours drinking, and even I'm starting to show the strain a little. She should at least be showing some signs of the general wear and tear of the day, it's just not natural. If I could bottle what she has I'd be a millionaire within days.

And yet, before I even have a chance to register properly what it is about her that draws me so forcefully to her, she's gone again. Maybe it's the mystery, the intrigue of not knowing anything about her? It's not just that she's attractive, as I have a very attractive woman in my arms already. But it's this other girl I really want, the mystery woman that I wish I could hold in my arms.

I don't understand what's happening to me.

Then it's 3am. The girl I've had in my arms for the last few hours and I have graduated to kissing and some pretty heavy petting, and it's looking like I'm going to be in for a damn good night when the drinking is finally over. We walk into a nightclub, myself, my friends, my new almost girlfriend.

And there she is. A vision of perfection in her purple blouse, black hair cascading over her shoulders, as she walks towards us, smiling and waving in greeting.

I can't help but stare at her. I know it's wrong, that I should be paying attention to the woman I have in my arms, but knowing this isn't good enough. I want her like I've never wanted any woman before. Just the sight of her is enough as she walks towards me, smiling.

Then she's gone, straight past me, not even a glance. She's talking to the guy who just came in behind us, and they're both looking very friendly, so maybe he's her boyfriend? And her arms are around him now, so he probably is her boyfriend.

I store this new knowledge of her, and realise that it's literally all I know about her. I still don't even know her name for Gods sake. We've been bumping into each other for nearly 18 hours now and I still don't know anything about her, except the fact she's probably unattainable.

I concentrate, focus my attention on the woman who is interested in me, the one I was kissing just a few moments ago. But I'm too late. The damage has been done. I can see that I have a lot of making up to do, and not enough time to do it in. It looks like I'm destined to spend the night in my hotel room after all.

Alone. Again.

She's there again today, at the football match. No sign of the boyfriend though, if he even was a boyfriend. She sat with us again, me and my friends that is, and once more nobody made any effort to introduce us. This is annoying, no, more

than annoying. I still don't know
anything about this girl.

Wait.

I know one thing about her - She likes football. The fact that
she's at a football match, wearing a football shirt, and a
football scarf, means that I can safely say she likes football.

Finally, there's something about this girl that I can actually
say I know.

I try to concentrate on the football. It's an important game
and I'm going to be a day late getting back to work because I
stayed to watch it. Except the game no longer matters, and
all that matters is her, just a few feet away, sitting there
looking wonderful.

I feel a nudge in my side, and turn in the direction it came
from. It's Helen, my new sort of girlfriend from Canada, who I
met 2 days ago whilst in Prague. She's gorgeous, we've just
had a great couple of days together, and she's already talking
about visiting England sometime soon.

And I'm ignoring her. Once more I have a beautiful woman at
my side, someone who truly likes me and is interested, and
once more I'm ignoring her in favour of a girl I don't know the
first thing about. I mentally kick myself in the nuts for being
so stupid and turn to
Helen, ready to devote myself to her.

"Who is she?"

A question from Helen, and I don't need to ask who she means.

"I don't know. She just keeps turning up and taking my breath away."

Bad answer. Good start, with the old 'I don't know' bit, but kind of lost it towards the end with the rest of it though. Telling your maybe girlfriend that a woman you don't know keeps showing up and taking your breath away is not good if you have any hopes of keeping said girl happy.

Except, Helen's different. She looks at the girl long and hard, and then turns back to me.

"Yes, I can see why you like her so much. She's stunning, and she always seems to be smiling, which is an improvement on most people. Just remember this though. You've been staring at her for the last 20 minutes, and either she hasn't noticed or she doesn't want to notice. Either way, from where I'm sitting she's out of your league. Now, I'm off to the little ladies room, and when I come back you better either be sitting with her and getting on like a house on fire or be sitting here waiting for me with a big apology and an even bigger
kiss."

I sit there and think to myself, which is difficult as I'm not very good at it and it tends to hurt a little. Actually, hurts a lot if I think too much.

So I try to keep my thinking simple. Pros and Cons, Helen versus Little Miss Mystery.

Little Miss Mystery

Pros. She's the most beautiful woman I ever saw.

Cons. That's all I know about her.

Helen

Pros. She's also beautiful. She's smart, she likes me a lot, we have a lot of fun together, she speaks the same language as me, she can drink almost as much vodka as I do, and she has a wonderful personality and a great sense of humour.

Cons. She's not Little Miss Mystery.

Or should that be a Pro? At least with Helen I know exactly what's on offer, and I know exactly what she wants in return, as opposed to knowing absolutely nothing about the other girl, and having no real likelihood of ever learning anything.

I notice Helen coming back up the steps towards me, but then she turns away slightly and heads over to Little Miss Mystery. She leans in and says something, then gets a reply. I notice them both giggling together, and I'm getting paranoid now. They both look in my direction, and then there's a little more laughter. What's going on? I don't know.

Then Helen comes back up towards me, smiling. I stand up to greet her and take her in my arms. We kiss, long and hard, both of us knowing that my obsession is over, and then Helen breaks off the kiss, smiles at me, and turns to whisper in my ear.

"Her names Nikol and she's getting married next month, but if she wasn't so in love she'd let you take her out for dinner. Unfortunately for you though, someone else got there first. And by the way, she spoke English all along!"

I look at Helen, turn to Nikol. She's looking at me with a big grin on her face. She waves at me, whispers the word 'sorry' in my direction, and points to her engagement ring which I somehow didn't notice in all the time I spent staring at her. And then all 3 of us start to laugh together.

I take hold of Helen again and start to kiss her, more passionately than I ever have before. At that moment there's a goal. 1-0 to Sparta Prague, which is the team I'm technically here to support, and everyone around us starts jumping up and down, celebrating.

I feel someone crash into me and turn around. It's Nikol, Little Miss Mystery. She grabs hold of me and kisses me, passionately, for what seems like an eternity. And then she lets go and whispers the words

"It was nice to meet you."

Then she's gone again. I turn back to Helen and she's laughing at me. We sit back down, me first, her on my lap. We're holding hands, laughing and joking together, and ignoring the football, just enjoying being together.

Life is good.

The Rapist

I say things you don't want to hear
Sometimes a whisper, sometimes more clear
I take the things you hold most dear
And hold them, savour them

You hate to see me, but you have no choice
The last thing you want to hear is my voice
I'm always there in the back of your mind
Searching for things you don't want me to find

Professionalism stops me from being too kind
My job is to hurt you, I hope you don't mind
I lurk in the shadows, the places you fear
A visit with me often induces tears

But one thing that I must make totally clear
You want me and need me

I can be there in the day, or in the night
Surprising you sometimes with clear insight
You hate me, you fear me, you think I'm a blight
On modern society, and maybe you're right

One thing I know and of this I am sure
If you didn't want me I wouldn't be here
I'll prey on your mind because that's what I do
I know that you think of me sometimes too

I know that you hate me, and always will do
But part of you knows that I'm helping you too
But time is now short and I have to leave

I know the time flies and I hope you don't grieve

The same time and place for our meeting next week
To continue your progress under my the-ra-py

The Bitter Hopes of Spring

It had been a harsh winter, the worst any of them could remember, but now, with the first scent of spring in the air the four survivors made their way outside, ready to begin the daily forage for food. Just on the other side of the hill in which they had made their shelter the remains of a town glistened in the snow, a reminder of when times had been much better for everyone.

Now there were only the four of them remaining, and although the sun was shining and the snow finally beginning to melt, one of them was still worried, perhaps even more worried now than she had been at any time during the winter that had just passed, when one by one most of their companions had died either of the cold or starvation, or a combination of the two.

Shyla had, in her mind anyway, a very good reason to be worried. She was the only female to have survived the winter, and while the males had been too busy trying to survive themselves to worry about anything else up until now, she knew that the spring would bring about a need for her to pick a mate. The main problem that she had with this was that it was going to leave the other two disappointed, and that could lead to conflict among the group.

She decided to make a suggestion in the hope that she could stave off the trouble she could sense would erupt in the group once she made her choice of mate. It was important to her that they continue to work together and remain close, as she knew another winter like this one would kill them all if they lost that camaraderie.

Calling to the other three Shyla put her proposal to them. She wanted to go and explore, look for other survivors. They couldn't be the only group to have made it through the winter, and they all knew that there was more safety for each of them if they could join a larger group. She didn't mention her main reasons for wanting to find another group though, as she felt it would be wiser to keep her own counsel on that for now.

Searching for other survivors would focus the guys minds on the task in hand, and would hopefully distract them from the fact that it was spring, the time of year when the urge to create new life was at its greatest, and of course the fact that there was only one female to go between them. She also hoped that they might find a group in which the females outnumbered the males, and so give the two that she would inevitably reject a chance to find someone else.

There was a brief discussion amongst them once she had stated her case, but it was clear to the others that her assertions were correct, and so before too much time had passed they were ready to begin their search. The main topic of discussion had been whether they should all go together, or whether they should try to search in different directions, meeting up back at the shelter each evening.

It was decided that it would be best to travel together, and to just pick one direction and try to keep to it as they would be sure to come across some signs of life eventually. Going out alone would be more dangerous. They were all well aware of how dangerous it could be out there, and even if they should find another group they might not be made welcome. Safety in numbers was the message preached continuously by Shyla, and the others saw the sense in her arguments.

It was still early morning when they set out on their trek, having first had a small breakfast of berries that they had saved from the previous evening. It wasn't the most appetizing way to begin a day, but with snow still on the ground it was difficult to find food sometimes. They were all confident that they would be able to find more as they searched though, and equally sure that they would be able to find somewhere to shelter when it got late and they were too tired to continue for the day.

As they ambled along, checking for signs of other survivors and any food that may be easily spotted from the path they were taking, Shyla assessed her three companions, knowing that this journey would only provide a temporary distraction to them and that she would be forced to choose a mate sooner or later.

They had always known one another and had similar upbringings, yet the three of them could not have been more different personality wise. The eldest was Jafan, although personality wise he was by far the least mature member of the group and was constantly playing pranks on the others. He was intelligent though, and was much better than the rest of them at finding food, and so they happily put up with his regularly idiotic and occasionally dangerous stunts.

Next there was Taye. He was the quiet one, and he liked to keep his own counsel on matters of importance to the group. When he did decide to raise his head above the parapet to voice an opinion, however, the others always listened to what he had to say. The general feeling in the group was that Taye would only speak when he absolutely had to, and then it was always in order to avoid someone in the group making a disastrous decision.

Finally there was Kito, who was constantly trying to make up for the fact that he was the youngest by trying to prove he was tougher and stronger than the others. His bravery was unquestionable, but he sometimes found himself in dangerous situations because of it, and had twice only been rescued from certain death by the timely arrival of Jafan. This, of course, only served to make him more determined to prove that he could get by without this assistance.

It was, as is often the case with the young, a never ending circle. He tried to prove himself, failed, and so became even more determined to try again.

No, he was too young, too rash, for Shyla to pick him as a mate. He may be stronger and faster than the other two, and obviously his youthful energy was fun to be around, but his never ending need to prove himself made him the least likely member of the group to survive in the long term, and if Shyla was going to pick a mate then she wanted it to be the one that could be there for their children in the long term.

This left a straight choice between Jafan or Taye, both of whom had very good qualities that would serve them well as potential parents. The problem though, was that although they were undoubtedly skilled at the more practical things, neither of them struck Shyla as long term mate material. Taye was too quiet, too reserved for her liking, and although

Jafan was fun to be around she was sure that his pranks would grow old on her after a while.

Plus, did she really want her children to have a role model that never really took anything seriously?

It was going to be a tough decision, whichever one she went for in the end. All she could do for now was to hope that ...

The attack came from nowhere. As the four companions came to the edge of a field, they started to follow the path into the wooded area beyond. They had barely gone a few feet into the gloom of the trees when Jafan, leading the group due to his seniority, heard a noise that he was familiar with but had hoped not to hear ever again, especially not here, today, as the group set out in the hope of finding others like them, fellow survivors.

Being the eldest, he had already reached the same conclusion as Shyla had about the group dynamics and how two of them were going to be disappointed. He didn't think that Taye and Kito had worked this out yet, although it was impossible to tell. Maybe the reason for Kito's rash bravado was because he was trying to catch the attention of Shyla and show that he was the best candidate for her to choose as mate, although nothing had ever been said.

As for Taye, the fact that he had never broached the subject meant nothing. He was renowned for keeping himself to himself. He was certainly very intelligent, but it was impossible to ever know what was going on in his mind.

Now, turning around at the sound of a scream, Jafan realized that any thoughts on the matter were now redundant. He had no idea where it had come from, as he had instinctively been heading into the wind in order to detect the scent of any such predator. Yet his senses had failed him, and as a result Shyla, that lovely young thing that he thought of almost like a daughter, had been taken.

There was no time for remorse now though. There could be a whole pack of them out there, and if so it meant the rest of them were in imminent danger as well. With a grunt of alarm that he knew was far too late to save Shyla he called the others to him, and the three remaining rabbits ran into the undergrowth, hoping to avoid any more foxes that might be out there.

The Morning After

It was going to be one of those days.

I knew as much as soon as I looked over towards what should have been a bleating alarm clock to instead see four red digits stridently flashing the fact that I was meant to have been in work over two hours ago in the direction of my sleepy gaze. This was not the first time I'd been late, and in fact lateness had become such a regular occurrence that I'd been warned the last time that one more episode of tardiness would result in my becoming gainfully unemployed.

I spent a few moments gazing at the offending clock, trying to decipher whether I had any grandparents I hadn't already killed off as an excuse for turning up so late, but knew deep down that there was nothing I could say that would convince my boss to keep me this time. It had just been one time too often for me to possibly hope to keep my job.

This was a shame, because I loved my job, or at least the money I earned, if only I could actually get my lazy ass out of bed in time to make it there and keep the damn thing. But there was nobody else to blame other than myself. I knew the night before that the vodka was a bad idea. It was always a bad idea, I just had a habit of convincing myself that it *wasn't* a bad idea at the time. I really should have known better, but the damage was done.

Now I had to make a decision. Did I actually bother getting out of bed, where I was feeling quite comfortable despite the after effects of the vodka, to make my way to a job I no longer had, or did I stay where I was and not bother? This, on the surface of it, should not have been a difficult choice, but deep down I was an eternal optimist and honestly believed on some level that no matter how bad things got there was a chance to rescue the situation.

Of course, turning up to work several hours late stinking of beer and vodka, especially when I'd been given more than ample notice of the fact that the next time would be the last was not, in fairness, the greatest way to try to turn things back in my favour.

And yet...

So I lay there and stared at the spinning ceiling. I had been awake for at least twenty minutes before I realized that one of the arms lying across my chest was not actually attached to me. This, even in my befuddled state, indicated that there was a fair probability that I had not spent the previous night alone, so now I also had to decide whether to move and risk disturbing the person lying beside me.

I knew from past experience that the probability was that the person I had slept with would not be a particularly attractive woman. I didn't have any idea how this happened so regularly, because to the best of my knowledge I'd never gone to bed with an ugly woman. But I did have a nasty habit of waking up beside them.

Part of me wondered if there was a certain kind of woman that liked to pick guys up in bars, take them home, use them and abuse them until they fell asleep, and then call up the biggest, fattest, and ugliest friend they knew and get them to switch places with them while the poor unsuspecting guy was asleep. I know that if I was an attractive woman I would probably do something like that just to fuck with guys heads.

But most people are not as twisted as me, so chances are my bizarre theory was nothing more than what it appeared to be, but still you could never be entirely sure. Women are devious creatures, after all, and as someone much more intelligent than me once said, you can't trust anyone that can bleed continuously for five days a month and not die.

Still, all that being said I was now lying there facing a double predicament. Did I get up to go to work or stay where I was? Did I risk disturbing the strange person beside me that I had still not yet even looked at, just in case she was really gruesome and insisted on some wake-up sex?

Decisions, decisions....

I contemplated things for a little while and deduced that the best course of action all round would probably be to go back to sleep. But that, in itself, risked causing more problems than it was worth.

In fairness, it wouldn't make much difference to my employment situation either way, so that wasn't something I really had to consider in making this decision. But by now, having been awake for a while, I was aware of the actual reason that I had come to from my drunken stupor.

I needed to go to the toilet.

This was not good, as it again left me in a position where I had to make one of two choices, neither of which were really envious at that moment. I could either get out of bed, in which case I would almost certainly wake the probable behemoth that was sleeping besides me with her arm draped across my chest in that worldwide female signal of ownership.

Or I could stay where I was, in which case I would almost certainly find myself lying in bodily fluids other than the traditional post-coital ones.

This actually wouldn't bother me all that much. It wouldn't be the first time I got drunk and pissed the bed, but there was a small chance that the person sharing my bed might not be a monster after all, in which case pissing all over the place would only serve to ensure I never got a chance of a repeat meeting with her.

Of course, I could just incline my head 45 degrees to the right to see who I had ended up in bed with this time, but that felt like it might be a little bit too much effort right now. Plus, for as long as all I was doing was staring up at the ceiling I could keep believing that I had gotten really lucky the night before and actually managed to entice a really nice girl back home with me.

Like pissing the bed, it wouldn't be the first time, even though sadly the occurrence that was the more regular of the two is not the one that I would want to boast about to my friends in the pub.

Anyway….

I lay there, staring at the ceiling, trying to decide which of the options open to me would be least likely to cause me pain, misery and/or untold suffering. Then I started trying to piece together the previous night in order to give myself a chance of working out which of the girls I had been talking to would be the most likely candidate to have become my early morning bed-partner.

There was Amy, who was super cute to look at but a little neurotic to talk to. Sara, who had been tending bar in my local, and who I knew had a crush on me but for some reason nothing had ever happened between us, probably because the only times I was ever confident enough to actually discuss the issue with her tended to be when I was in no fit state to physically do anything other than drool over her.

There had also been a myriad other girls that I had spoken to, and all of them had been really good looking, but that was normal. This was, after all, one of the reasons I'd chosen to move to the Czech Republic in the first place. Even the plain Czech girls were stunning when compared to English women.

Unfortunately, the other selling point for the country had been the fact that beer was cheaper than water, which seemed like a good thing at the time, but after a few years had turned me into a drunken idiot. Although, in fairness, I hadn't really needed much encouragement to bring out either my inner drunk or my inner idiot, both of whom had been trying to break free for quite some time before I made the move.

Moving here had just helped to facilitate their escapes.

None of these ruminations, of course, succeeded in helping me to deal with my current predicament. My body was now making it very clear that if I didn't do something about offering it relief shortly it would be taking matters into its own hands, so to speak. That would not bode well for me if it was Sara lying beside me, as she wasn't the only one of us with an unrequited crush and if I had finally managed to get her here it would give me the confidence to believe that I could do it again at a later date.

Unless I pissed all over her of course, as then my amorous intentions towards her would be over with for sure. Unfortunately for me she wasn't German, as I'd heard tales that they were the race that would be most likely to enjoy an early morning yellow water wake up call.

After lying there for a few more minutes my bladder began sending out an SOS signal, informing me that I had about 45 seconds before it was going to empty itself, and thus forced me to make an immediate decision with regards my plans for the morning.

Moving the arm from across my chest as gently as I could in the circumstances I climbed out of bed and headed toward the toilet. It was at this point that something I should have realized much earlier became evident. I was not, as my befuddled mind had thus far been surmising, actually in my own bed, room, or even flat.

How this detail had failed to register in the 35 minutes or so I had already been awake was completely beyond my ability to compute at that moment. The important thing was trying to work out an efficient route to the little boys room, preferably before it was too late to be necessary, and with luck also get there without accidentally bumping into anybody my as yet unidentified bed partner might be living with.

This had actually happened once in Austria, when I'd stumbled out of the room of a very attractive young lady, again for an early morning emergency ablution, only to bump into the girls father in the hallway. The fact that I hadn't bothered to spend a few seconds to put any clothes on in my haste probably did not make for a great first impression. That I was asked to leave shortly after by my partner for the night as her family had to go to church due to the fact her mother was the local Pastor was something that I had always found to be fairly ironic.

After all, she was 17 years old and her dad had seen me wandering around the house naked an hour earlier. Chances are the sermon that morning would have been aimed directly at the young girl sitting in the front pew, although I didn't stay around to find out.

I digress however, which coincidentally was exactly what I was doing as I wandered around the strange apartment trying to work out which of the various doorways protected the home of the porcelain throne. The act of starting to move around had seemingly been enough to sufficiently change the position of the liquid in my bladder slightly and reduce its need to escape from Defcon 1 to Defcon 2, meaning I still had a few moments to investigate my surroundings and try to make the correct doorway decision.

I initially found myself faced with three possible routes to the redemption of my impending bladder evacuation. Noticing posters of some generic pop stars on one doorway I immediately deduced this room to be the nesting place of a younger member of the human race, which thus left me with a choice of two portals to penile relief.

A second door, upon a tentative investigation, was found to lead to the kitchen, which of course only left me with one more option, or so I thought. By now I was, of course, rapidly re-approaching a critical phase of my future bladder management and so went through the third door as though my life depended on it, only to find I was standing in another bedroom which contained a mid-coital couple who were clearly somewhat underwhelmed by my sudden interruption of their passionate embrace.

I vaguely recognized the female member of the couple as Amy, one of the girls that had been on my mental check-list of potential bed-partners, and seeing her in action with her chosen partner made it clear that I should have ignored her mildly annoying personality and pursued her a little more vigorously than I evidently had done the night before.

But it was too late for that now, and with dual cries of 'fuck off you pervert' resonating from the other side of the room I closed the door in a state of bemused perplexation as I tried to deduce where the room of relief might be situated in this strange apartment.

My musings were interrupted by the unmistakable sound of movement coming from the room I had so recently vacated in order to begin my meander through the seemingly lavatory-less lodging, implying that my bed-partner was almost certainly awake and was probably wondering where I had escaped to, unless of course her head was as fuzzy as mine was and she had no recollection of bringing me home with her last night.

This thought raised the intriguing possibility of me finding somewhere to hide until she went out somewhere, or possibly just until she went into another room, at which point I could attempt to rescue my clothes and escape undetected. Then I remembered that my clothes were still in her room, which would mean she would probably see them soon enough, so my chances of a safe getaway were remote.

Having discarded this idea I went back to concentrating on the issue at hand, which was the serious need to relieve myself before I made a mess of the hallway carpet. The movement in the other room was becoming more pronounced and I knew it would only be a matter of moments before the person with whom I had spent the night came looking for me, and so in desperation I ran into the kitchen as soundlessly as possible and took care of the business that had initially roused me from my slumber as rapidly as I could, using the sink as an emergency portal for my morning ministrations.

I was barely finished with what I was doing when my nocturnal nookie partner entered the kitchen to find me sitting at the kitchen table with my head held in my hands in the universal signal of regretful over-indulgence. I wasn't really paying much attention as she walked through the door, wanting to delay the inevitable feelings of

"What the hell was I thinking when I came home with that?"

which I was sure would be forthcoming just as soon as I saw for sure what type of creature my drunkenness had paired me up with this time, so it wasn't until she spoke that I realized who I had spent the night with, and at that point I allowed myself a brief moment of hope.

"Hey Steve," said Jennifer, my bitchy but extremely cute boss. "I guess I can forgive you for not making it to work on time this morning, seeing as I'm not there either".

Her tone was warm and pleasant, and I actually found myself feeling much more pleased with my situation that I had been just a few moments later. I looked up and flashed her a smile, trying to blow the cobwebs away from my brain, knowing that there was something really important that I was forgetting, and certain that this morning friendliness from a woman who had been figuratively riding me for months, and seemingly literally riding me last night, would not last much longer unless I could remember whatever it was that was trying to push itself to the front of my befuddled mind.

As is often the case in such situations, the missing piece of information managed to make its way through the defenses of my mind and plant itself front and center and ready for inspection exactly 27 milliseconds after it became a moot point.

Jennifer had spent the last minute or so pottering around the kitchen, clearly getting prepared to have her first coffee of the day, when disaster struck, and I knew instantly that not only was I fired after all, there would certainly be no chance of a repeat performance with the woman all the lads at work had dubbed the Ice Queen.

She looked at me, brown eyes wide in shock and disgust, before spitting out the words that in the back of my mind I had dreaded from the moment she walked into the room.

"Steve," she began, seemingly in shock and trying to force the words to make the journey from her brain to her mouth, and then out into the world where everyone else could hear them.

"Please fucking tell me that you didn't take a shit in my kitchen sink?"

Valentines Meal

Valentines Day, and in less than an hour I was going to meet my girlfriend in the most expensive restaurant in town. I'd never been so nervous about anything in my entire life, unsure about how she was going to react when I said what I so wanted, no, needed to say to her.

I had wanted to do this for months, and now the moment was almost upon me I was having second thoughts. Sitting in the bath I was trying to work out how best to word things, with all of the different scenarios running through my head, and sure of nothing any more apart from my feelings.

And, to be honest, right now not even all that certain about them.

How hard could it be? I thought, as I stepped out of the bath and started to towel myself dry. It was only a few short words. There couldn't be anything too complicated about it. Say what you want to say and wait for the response. After that, obviously, I was going to have to wing it.

There was no way of knowing in advance what her reaction would be. I knew which one I wanted, and there was a chance it could happen. My girlfriend and I had been going out for nearly five years now, so I knew her as well as I was ever likely to and could predict how she would behave in all but the most unpredictable of circumstances.

And this was not what I would have classed as unpredictable. She knew that over the last year or so we'd been gradually getting closer together, spending more and more time with each other, seeing movies together, and taking daytrips and walks in the country and so on.

Surely the next logical step had occurred to her as well by now.

Even so, I was worried. Panicking even, feeling the sweat starting to form on the palms of my hands even before I'd finished drying them from getting out of the bath. Knowing that in this state whatever I wore I was going to look a nervous wreck by the time I got to the restaurant.

Also knowing that there was nothing I could do that would make me calm myself down. I was just going to have to do the best I could and hope she didn't notice how worried I was before it was the right time.

The right time...was there ever a right time for something like this? When I had thought about it over the last couple of months this had seemed like the perfect plan. Or, if not perfect, the nearest I was ever likely to get to perfect. Yet now, just half an hour before I was due to meet her, I was having second thoughts.

I prepared myself a glass of vodka and tried to push the doubts to the back of my mind, tried to convince myself that this was the right time to do this, to finally make the commitment and let everyone know how I felt about her. As I waited for the taxi that would transport me to the rendezvous with my girlfriend though I just wasn't sure it was a good idea any more.

I poured myself another vodka, being a little more generous with the measure this time, as I thought one last time about what I was planning to do. I weighed up the good and the bad of the options available to me, trying to come to the right decision before it was too late.

Then, as I downed the vodka in one I stopped worrying. I knew I was doing the right thing, and that she felt the same way I did. As the taxi driver pulled up outside with a blast of his horn I headed for the door, and the date with my girlfriend, feeling much more confident about things.

It seemed like just a few seconds, when in reality it was nearly fifteen minutes later, when the taxi pulled up outside the restaurant. I was a few minutes early, and after tipping the driver and wishing him a good evening I prepared myself for the inevitable wait for Sue, my girlfriend to arrive.

A wait which was nowhere near as long as I was used to, as within a couple of minutes Sue came around the corner, with Julie, her divorced mother in tow.

I know most guys would have blanched at seeing the two women approach, girlfriend and mother, on a night like tonight. I was used to it though as Julie had come along with Sue most of the times we'd gone out since the divorce had been finalised last January.

My heart skipped a beat when I saw them coming towards me, and the earlier panic started to resurface suddenly. One look though, one sideways glance from her in my direction, and I knew that I was right. She was definitely the woman for me.

We walked into the restaurant and took our seats almost immediately, making small talk as is customary in such situations until the food and drinks had been ordered and the waiter had left us alone.

Sue and Julie started discussing some inane TV show as the waiter walked away, and I tuned myself out of the conversation for a few moments while trying to work out when was the best time to make my announcement.

Was it best to say something once our drinks were served? Or should I wait until after the soup, the main course, or even dessert? Should I speak whilst we were eating, or wait until all the formalities had been taken care of when everyone would be feeling sated, happy, and content with their lot?

I was so intent in concentration that I didn't even realise that Sue had asked me the question, until she repeated it that is.

"So, Jason, is there any special reason for you inviting me out here, the most expensive, most romantic place in town, on Valentine's Night?"

I could see a glint in her eyes, in both their eyes in fact. She had never looked as happy as she did now in all the time I'd known her.

I took a breath and prepared to say what it was I had come here to say. What I'd been waiting to say for all of these months. I closed my eyes as I tried to think of the best way to phrase things, all the time feeling two pairs of eyes on me, knowing that they were waiting patiently for me to reply.

I knew this was my last chance, the final moment when I could change my mind, shake my head and pretend there was nothing special that I had to say. I also knew that to do so would be to go against what I wanted, what I truly believed in.

I opened my eyes and looked across the table, at Sue, my girlfriend, and Julie, her mother, and could feel the expectation being sent back across towards me. This was it, my moment, the point of no return.

"Sue, honey, we've been together for five years now, and it's been probably the best, most enjoyable five years of my life." At this point I changed the direction of my gaze slightly before continuing with what I had to say, the speech that I knew one way or another was going to change so much.

"Over the last year or so we've become closer than we'd ever been before, closer than I would have believed possible to be honest. We've spent so much more time together than we could previously, gotten to know each other much more intimately than we ever did before. Now I feel it's time to make that final commitment to each other, to take it that step further."

I sensed both women opposite me take a breath just before I finished.

"Julie, would you do me the honour of being my wife?"

Authors Notes

This is the part of the book where I waste your time telling you where the inspiration for the stories/tales/poems in this book came from. Or didn't come from in some cases. Feel free to read this section or skip right through it, depending on your personal preference, I won't be offended/overjoyed either way. But for those of you that might be into this kind of thing, have at it and enjoy.

Sunday Afternoon Drive

This story, remarkably, is mostly true. Except for the driving part, that never happened. But I was in Prague with a friend, we did get drunk, and he did mistake a cute German girl for a urinal. As the saying goes, with friends like these...

Taken

This was originally intended to be a novel, or at least a much longer story than it ended up becoming. The plan was to write a story of a kidnapping from the perspective of the kidnapper, then I suddenly came up with a rather strange twist at the end and decided it worked better that way. Plus I realized I was too lazy to write a whole novel...

The Chair

This one scares me a little. I was actually asleep and was woken with a sudden urge to write this. I later found out that at the exact moment I woke up, a friend of mine was in the back of an ambulance and coding after a suicide attempt. She recovered fully, fortunately, but the fact that I felt such a need to write something on this subject at that moment has always freaked me out...

The Cavalier

This story came about as the result of a competition that was being run by a website. They gave the first line, and I had to come up with the rest. It took about 10 minutes to write, so clearly not much thought went into it, but I think it turned out okay...

Bomb Damaged Lager

Another true story, and one of the longest days of my life. Nothing in here is embellished or made up, it's just a factual account of the aftermath of the biggest bomb ever exploded on UK soil. Miraculously, nobody was killed in the blast, and it's been argued since by many people, including myself, that the bomb was probably one of the best things that ever happened to the city due to the money that was pumped in to regenerate the place afterwards...

Trust

An online friend told me some things about her past and asked me to write a story based on what she told me. I don't know if I did her tale justice or not, but she seemed happy enough with it at the time…

Ode to Frog

I was feeling silly and may have partaken of a beer or two. This is what sometimes happens when those things happen simultaneously…

Addiction

I have no idea where this came from, or why. It just appeared on my computer screen one afternoon when I was trying to write an email…

One Good Cigarette

I was in a hostel in Prague and stayed there for about a week, and there was a guy there at the same time who always had a cigarette behind his ear. I never saw him smoke, not even once, so was puzzled about why the cigarette was there. Then this came spewing out of me the day before I was due to fly home…

The Lidless Eye

Not one of my best tales in fairness, and another competition entry. All I was given here was the title and a word count that I couldn't exceed. I do like the little touch of horror in the last sentence though...

Being Cool is Easy

A rare attempt at poetry for me, inspired by seeing some idiots ganging up and bullying someone just because he wore glasses. Right after I got in their faces and told them to pick on someone their own size...

Donors

Before escaping from the UK I used to donate blood regularly. I rode a motorbike and figured that one day I'd probably crash and need some serious help, so it was only right and proper that I have some of my own blood available just in case. And one day as I was lying there a cute girl walked in. We never spoke, but it was enough to put this silly idea in my head...

Consequences

Sometimes I sit down to check emails or do some work, and stories appear. This is one of those. No back story, no inspiration, just the sudden appearance of a short story when I was least expecting it...

Hijack

I used to go past Manchester Airport all the time on my motorbike and regularly saw planes coming into land just a couple of hundred feet above me. I also found it strange that aerosols were allowed on flights when bottles of water weren't. So I put two and two together and came up with this...

The Reaper

One of the few attempts I've made at poetry that I actually quite like. I was having a bad day and feeling miserable, and wondering how and why the universe chooses the time and circumstances of each individual death, because I'm just strange like that. And then this was sitting there on the screen in front of me suddenly...

Conspiracy Theory

Inspired by waking up next to yet another bushpig after a drinking binge. I don't think any more needs to be said...

Hit and Run

Like Taken, I wanted to write something from the perspective of the person that's doing something wrong. I was halfway through before I thought it would be cool to have him going to the funeral of his son. It appealed to my sense of irony...

Old Albert

When I was a kid we actually did have a harvest festival at school, and I did recommend an old couple from across the street for a food parcel. And for a while I talked to them whenever I saw them out and about, but as often happens I lost touch with them over time. This is my idealized version of what MIGHT have happened in other circumstances...

Rebecca

Another competition entry, again, with only the first line as inspiration. This was written at a time when internet dating was still a fairly new thing, and it was my way of looking at this new phenomenon and trying to understand the reasons that people might have, and the emotions they might go through...

Too Young

A friend told me she thought her 15 year old niece might be pregnant. And then this happened a few minutes later...

Sexist Theory

Since I first put this up online I've had a bunch of people give me crap over it because of how stereotypical it is. Which of course was the point. Irony people – It's not just a way to describe a slightly rumpled shirt...

Coffee Stains

A friend approached me at work with a sentence written on a piece of paper as inspiration for a story. Also written on that piece of paper was the phrase 'Sorry about the coffee stains', which had seemingly appeared on said piece of paper after he accidentally used it as a coaster ten minutes before heading to work. I preferred that to the original sentence, and this was the result...

I Hate Umbrellas

This is a fact, I genuinely hate the fucking things. And this was my way of trying to explain why...

Vengeance

Much more of this is true than I would like. I did have a friend at work, she was treated in the way described in this tale, and I did wait outside the company offices a year or so later with a plan to give the guy responsible what he deserved. Fortunately (probably for me and him both), he left work with a few colleagues that night and went to the pub, and as it was winter I really couldn't be bothered sitting around outside for the next five hours waiting for him...

Tunnel of Death

This was inspired by a visit to Terezin, a small town outside of Prague that was used as a Gestapo prison during the Second World War. There's a medieval fortress there that has a tunnel running through the walls from the barracks area to what was used as the place of execution. And that tunnel is extremely tight and winding, and not a place to go if you have claustrophobia. I wrote this a week or so later when I got home...

Janie's Got a Gun

Inspired by the Aerosmith song and accompanying video. Nothing more needs to be said I think...

Don't Cry

Another one inspired by a song. It was originally supposed to be about a guy whose girlfriend left him, but then of course my mind had other plans. I kind of like the twist at the end, and I hope you do too...

Hallowed be Thy Name

Iron Maiden's classic song inspired this tale of a man waiting for his execution...

Axe Murder

Truth be told I have no idea where this came from. It just appeared in my mind one afternoon about 4 seconds before it appeared on the screen in front of me...

A Week of Tearing Up

This was written as a challenge for a writers group I set up in Prague. One of my friends came up with the title, and I came up with the idea of a foster child about to leave home and join the real world for the first time. And then I came up with another idea right at the end...

Obsession

Another one of those tales on this list that is partly true. I'll let you work out which parts are real and which parts just figments of my imagination...

The Rapist

I guess being European I'll never be able to understand the American obsession with therapy. I'm sure it's helpful for some people, but when you have five your old kids with a therapist then there's clearly something wrong with society. I guess this was my way of pointing out that maybe this obsession stems from people being mind-raped into thinking it's more normal than it really is, and the only people that would benefit from such a thing are the people making money out of it...

The Bitter Hopes of Spring

I always kind of wanted to write an 'after the apocalypse' kind of story, and that's what this was, at least until my brain twisted it at the last minute that is. I think it works well though, and is one of my rare attempts at actual character study in a short story...

The Morning After

I'm not sure what was going through my mind when I wrote this, but for the record I haven't ever taken a dump in a kitchen sink, or any other kind of sink for that matter. And as far as I know none of my friends have either. Sometimes my imagination scares me a little with what comes out of it, and this was one of those occasions...

Valentines Meal

As an almost perpetually single guy I get fed up with all the crap that surrounds Valentines Day each year. So I decided to write a story that shows my disdain for the whole forced romance thing...

Dedication

There are a bunch of people I want to thank, as without them this book might never have happened, and certainly wouldn't have happened twice!

Firstly, thank you to everyone that has ever encouraged my writing. Writing is one of the most lonely things it's possible to do, and having people out there telling you that you're doing a decent job, or at least not screwing up too badly, is a must for any writer. Your encouragement is truly appreciated, even if we don't always say it as clearly as we might.

Secondly, thank you to the Prague Writers Group, especially Sonya Lano, for many years of helpful advice, constructive criticism, and editing work. Again, I may not always show it, but every moment of effort you've put in to try to help me improve as a writer is appreciated more than you can ever know.

Over the years there are certain writers whose books have resonated with me more than any others, and as such these people have no doubt influenced my writing in some way or another. So even though they'll almost certainly never see this, especially the dead ones, thank you to Stephen King, J.R.R. Tolkien, Douglas Adams, Terry Pratchett, and Markus Zusak, to name just a few, for dragging me into your own worlds and inspiring me to try to drag people into mine.

Thanks also to the musicians that have inspired me over the years, and most especially to Marah, the Last Great Rock and Roll Band, for allowing me to join you guys on so many adventures over the years. Without you guys and your music, there would be a hole in my life that I would never be able to plug...

Of course I can't leave out my family, without whose support I wouldn't be in the position I'm in now. So thank you to my sisters, for their support in all aspects over the years, but especially for the support showed when I left the UK with my tail between my legs and my spirit as close to broken as it's ever been. I'm not the kind of person that does the soppy stuff very well, but without you guys who knows how dark things might have gotten for me...

I should also say thank you to Ian, referred to in this book as my 'Evil Step Dad'. Ian was a person that I never got on with, and that was mostly due to my own stubbornness to realise that the stubbornness I was displaying actually came from him. He's called the Evil Step Dad in this book, but right here is where I'm going to call him what I was too stupid to call him when he was alive – my true father, my Dad...

I can't finish this page without a mention of my brother, Darrel, who was cruelly taken from us when he was still practically just a kid. He was the black sheep of the family in some ways, but was such a cheeky little scamp that nobody could ever stay mad at him forever, and he had a true heart of gold...

And finally, this book, and everything else I do, is dedicated to the memory of the most amazing person I ever met, my mother. The best friend I ever had, the person that was always there for me no matter what I did, and the person I aspire to be like as I get older. A true inspiration to everyone she ever met, and the biggest single influence on everything I've ever done. Gone, but never forgotten…

Printed in Great Britain
by Amazon